SCORCHING DESIRE
TRINITY MASTERS: FALL OF THE GRAND MASTER
BOOK THREE

MARI CARR

LILA DUBOIS

Copyright 2017 by Mari Carr and Lila Dubois

All Rights Reserved.

No part of this book, with the exception of brief quotations for book reviews or critical articles, may be reproduced or transmitted in any form or by any means, electronic or mechanical, including photocopying, recording, or by any information storage and retrieval system without express written permission from the author.

This is a work of fiction. Names, characters, places, and incidents are the product of the author's imagination or are used fictitiously, and any resemblance to actual persons, living or dead, business establishments, events, or locales is entirely coincidental.

Editor: Kelli Collins

Cover artist: Lila Dubois

❋ Created with Vellum

TRIGGER WARNINGS

The Trinity Masters series is a romantic suspense and all books contain explicit sex and depictions of violence (action scenes).

SCORCHING DESIRE

A reformed spy. A modern-day rake. And a man with too many secrets.

When Damon Corso is blackmailed it's not just his career that's in jeopardy, but the existence of the Trinity Masters—America's oldest and most powerful secret society. He and fellow member Marco Polin, a world famous playboy musician, enjoy sharing women, a secret that until now they've kept quiet.

Tasha Kasharin, the spy sent to help them, knows this is more than simple blackmail. Marco and Damon's lives are in danger. She ignores her increasingly vivid fantasies about being part of a trinity with them until their investigation is interrupted by the Grand Master, who calls them to the altar and binds them in a *ménage* marriage.

The men must trust their futures to the unexpectedly innocent woman who's now their wife, while dealing with the change in their own relationship, and the complicated feelings that come with it. Blackmail escalates to violence, and they'll have to trust and accept one another if they're going to survive.

CHAPTER ONE

He'd put them all in danger.

Damon put his hand in his pocket and formed a fist, trying to hide his anger. He had no one to be angry at but himself.

"You understand what's at stake." The Grand Master sat in shadow, only his right hand, which lay on the desk, visible. They were in the secret headquarters of the Trinity Masters, deep under the Boston library.

"I do, Grand Master." Damon couldn't stand still. He paced the private office. "I'll resign."

"And how will that benefit the Trinity Masters?"

"I'll resign from everything, including the Trinity Masters."

"Mr. Corzo, I think you forget who we are. You do not leave the Trinity Masters."

Damon turned away, examining the shadowy corners of the office. The Trinity Masters were America's oldest and most powerful secret society. Formed as the states were uniting in rebellion, the first leaders sought to strengthen their new nation through alliances between powerful and important people. They used the arranged marriages to connect influential families, captains of industry and religious leaders. But it wasn't just two people they united, it was three.

In modern times, becoming a member meant access to some of the most powerful and innovative thinkers in the country. If you were selected to join you were guaranteed to rise far and fast. The Trinity Masters counted politicians, CEOs, Nobel Prize winning scientists and world-renowned artists among their ranks. The Grand Master of the Trinity Masters helped the members excel in their chosen profession or field, and when the time came, he called them to the altar and matched them with two others in a trinity marriage.

At twenty-seven, Damon was already an Assistant U.S. Attorney, the third step in a six-part fifteen-year plan to put him on the federal bench. He'd joined the Trinity Masters in college. It hadn't made his life easier. Instead, it had pushed him to work harder, to excel each step of the way.

And knowing that he would someday be part of an arranged marriage meant he had taken full advantage of the fact he didn't need to worry about dating or relationships.

That had led to his current problem.

"Your friendship with Marco Polin was unusual, but not problematic." The Grand Master tapped his fingers on the top of his desk. "Until now."

"I know, Grand Master."

"There are several legal options." Damon rubbed his eyebrow. "But almost all of them would then require the video be entered into evidence. We could try to limit access to the evidence. The likelihood that anyone who sees the video would make the connection between Marco and I and the Trinity—"

"Is an unacceptable risk. Your rings are clearly visible. It would be far too easy for someone to start wondering why an

Assistant U.S. Attorney and a famous cellist were wearing matching rings while they fucked the same woman."

Damon hung his head.

Taking advantage of his freedom until he was called to the altar had included indulging in every sexual desire and kink that ever interested him. His job required him to be circumspect with his personal life. But luckily, Marco Polin—a college friend who was also in the Trinity Masters—was a famous musician with the elegant playboy lifestyle that only classical musicians could pull off. For years Damon had been attending Marco's parties, which had the tendency to devolve into orgies, to indulge himself.

This time they'd been caught on tape. The blackmail video had shown up in his personal email three days ago. He'd immediately gotten in touch with the Grand Master, who'd ordered him to Boston.

"Tell me again, how many people were at the party?"

"When the video was taken? Ten, maybe. They were all women except for Marco and I."

"An enjoyable sex party."

"It wasn't like that..." The protest was lame. It had been exactly like that. It was hardly his fault that he enjoyed sexy, adventurous women. And when the one Marco was fucking had beckoned him over so she could suck his cock, who was he to stand in the way of a lady's pleasure?

"How did these women come to be at the party?"

"I'm not sure." Despite the seriousness of the situation, Damon's lips twitched. "Marco attracts beautiful women."

"This is risky behavior."

"Don't worry, we're both on the new experimental STD vaccines."

"How thrilling that you're taking advantage of your fellow Trinity Master's scientific advancements."

Damon was a respected and aggressive attorney, a fearless human-rights activist and an expert pugilist. The Grand Master made him feel like a stupid teenager.

"Grand Master, I deeply regret what I've done and the trouble it's caused you and the Trinity Masters. The blackmailer didn't mention the matching rings—they just want money. I'll quit the Trinity Masters and pay the blackmailer. I will, of course, still help you in any way you ask. I will remain a friend to the Trinity Masters."

The Grand Master picked up a letter opener and balanced it on the top of the desk. It didn't escape Marco that it was shaped like a sword.

"Many of our members have helped you get where you are today. I don't discount your abilities—you're unique in your passion and remarkable in your skills, but neither will I discount our efforts to accelerate your career. You would be a valuable addition to the justice system."

The Grand Master sat forward, his strong face visible by the light of the single desk lamp. Damon noticed just a trace of weariness in the man's eyes that surprised him. However, that brief sign of weakness was soon replaced with a hard expression that said the Grand Master would not be crossed.

"Perhaps you've forgotten why our society exists. We protect the United States, we ensure that the best and the brightest rise to protect the ideals of our great nation. You're part of that plan. We need you on the bench as a federal judge."

"Yes, Grand Master." Damon bowed his head.

"I will send someone to assist you with the situation. I expect your full attention until this is resolved."

"I have to be in court in ten days, sir."

"Then you have a deadline. I will contact you."

Damon looked at the Grand Master, waiting to hear what the plan was or who he would send to help them. From his time as a prosecutor and working in a private firm, Damon knew that blackmail was infamously unreported, precisely because by its very nature it meant that the victim couldn't, or wouldn't, go to the authorities. The situation would have been bad enough for him personally and professionally even without the added complication of his actions putting the secret of the Trinity Masters in jeopardy.

"Goodbye, Mr. Corzo."

Damon raised one brow. There was no mistaking that dismissal.

He made his way out of the Trinity Masters' headquarters, taking the secret elevator to the rare-book room in the back of the Boston Library. He pulled his phone from his pocket as he walked.

"Marco," he said when his friend picked up. "I just met with the GM. I'm coming to Chicago."

He booked a flight on his phone as he hailed a cab. All he could hope was that the Grand Master had some very good tricks up his sleeve.

THE GRAND MASTER swiveled his chair, staring into the shadows in the corner.

"Well?" he asked.

Natasha Kasharin stepped from the darkness into the light. She wore slim black pants and a white button-down shirt, which should have been simple, nearly androgynous attire. But she looked more sexual than another woman would in lingerie, and more dangerous than a Navy SEAL in full gear.

"You heard?" he asked her.

Natasha, who went by Tasha, cocked her head to the side,

blonde hair falling against her cheek. "Blackmailed at an orgy? How original."

The Grand Master's lips twitched. Tasha was witty and fun, but few people had an opportunity to see it. Natasha's life had been anything but easy—her membership in the Trinity Masters was meant to correct that, to give her safety and a chance at a meaningful, if not exactly traditional, relationship.

Though she was American by birth, she was the daughter of two KGB agents and had been raised to be a spy for Russia. At the age of twelve she'd turned herself in to the CIA and spent high school as a double agent, reporting on her own parents' activities.

Her patriotism had come at a terrible cost, and when her CIA handler—a Trinity Masters member—retired, he'd helped Tasha get out of the spy business and made sure she became a member of their society.

The Grand Master had wanted to respect his old friend's request that Tasha be given a life worthy of her sacrifice, but she was too skilled and valuable a resource for him to ignore. In the five years since she'd been a member, she'd cleaned up messes, taken down those who stood in their way and retrieved information they needed.

He'd used her the same way her parents had. The same way the CIA had.

As much as he might want to stick to his ideals, the Grand Master couldn't ignore the sharpest weapon in his arsenal. There were men and women who were more dangerous, more powerful. They were guns—violent and hot, or knives—sharp and cold. Tasha was a syringe full of poison—silent, deadly and unnoticed until it was too late. And unlike the others he considered dangerous, Tasha had nothing to lose.

"I will talk to him first," she said. "He is lying about something."

"It wouldn't surprise me. He'll go to Chicago. Marco has a place there."

"The other man in the video?"

"Yes."

"Good, I will talk to both of them." She walked toward the door.

"Tasha."

"Yes?" She didn't turn, but her steps paused.

"Don't kill anyone."

She turned her head just enough for him to see the curve of her cheek. "There are so many things worse than death."

The Grand Master stared at the closed door of his office for a long time after she left.

CHAPTER TWO

Marco Polin ran through Chopin's *Scherzo No. 2 Op. 31*.

"For God's sake," Damon muttered. He brought a coaster over and set it on the edge of the baby grand where Marc had propped his drink. "Use a damned coaster. And play something else. I'm sick of that piece."

"You'll make an excellent wife," Marco told his best friend, ignoring the request to change pieces. Playing calmed him, and *Scherzo No. 2* was complicated enough that he had to concentrate. There was no space in his head to worry about their current predicament.

"I'm not going to defend you in court when you're sued for ruining that piano by using it as a table." Damon was pacing, a sure sign he was stressed. His hair was mussed, the light-brown strands disheveled, which was very unlike Damon.

"It's my piano." Marco shifted to the right as the key changed.

"No, it's not. It's on loan to you."

Marco snorted. "You worry too much."

"How much is that thing worth again?"

"This piano?" Marco pounded through a crescendo, feeling the music swell through him. "Most likely it's priceless. Charles Walter only makes sixty pianos a year."

When Damon didn't say anything more, Marco looked over his shoulder. His best friend was standing at one of the glass walls, looking out over the Chicago skyline. Damon's two-story condo with reinforced floors that allowed him to have the piano, had a good, if not excellent, view. Of all his homes—London, Singapore and Chicago—this condo was his favorite. It felt the most like home.

And one of the reasons it felt like home was staring out the window. Though Damon was now based in Los Angeles at the US Attorney's office there, he'd been living in Chicago working for a litigation firm before that. Those few years, when he and Damon had lived together, enjoying the many amenities available to the young and wealthy, had been some of Marco's happiest.

He doubted Damon knew that, and he would never tell him. Damon wasn't tormented by emotions the way Marco was—a trait Marco both envied and pitied. The closeness they shared was precious to Marco, but he suspected telling Damon that would make the other man uncomfortable.

"Who do you think they'll send?" Marco asked.

"Price Bennett is a member. I heard someone mention his name at one of the annual meetings."

"They're parties, not meetings." Marco shook his head. Only Damon would call a costumed masquerade a meeting. "And who is Price Bennett?"

"Seriously? He's CEO of Bennett Securities and heir to one of the largest fortunes in North America. The guy's richer than Trump, extremely well connected and the one to call if you need someone to watch your back. I'd be surprised if the guy didn't break the equivalent of this generation's Watergate scandal in his lifetime. He's got eyes and ears everywhere. The only problem is I understand he was recently matched. For all we know he could be out of the country on his honeymoon. I hope to God he's not."

Marco finished the piece with a flourish and then closed the key cover of the piano. "Because he could help us?"

"Maybe. I don't know. How do you stop a blackmailer?"

Marco picked up his drink and carried it—and the coaster—to the window. Slinging his free arm around Damon's shoulders, he took a sip. "I don't know. I'm afraid my faith in humanity is broken."

"We knew we were playing with fire."

"Ah, but what's the point if you aren't risking a burn?"

Damon's jaw clenched and his shoulders went rigid, but then he relaxed. "I want to be pissed at you, but it's hard."

"Why would you be mad at me?"

"Because you have terrible taste in women."

"I have excellent taste in women." Marco took Damon's glass and went to the wet bar to make them fresh drinks.

"If you did, one of them wouldn't be blackmailing me."

"I didn't realize you expected me to find us women who are beautiful, sexually adventurous and moral."

"If anyone could find them you could." Damon accepted his glass and raised it in salute.

"Next time I'll be more selective." Marco took a sip and then wandered over to the massive white-leather couch that dominated his living room.

"I doubt there will be a next time," Damon said, following Marco over.

"Why? I'm sure this will be fixed."

"You have a lot of faith."

"Do you doubt the Trinity Masters' power?" Marco had no

illusions about his skill as a musician—he was exceptionally gifted, yet there were hundreds, maybe thousands, of people with his same skill level who did not enjoy his career and international fame. The Trinity Masters had been his patrons, putting him in front of the right people at the right times. Marco's belief in the organization was absolute.

"No, but I think there are some situations even they can't fix."

"That's true."

Marco jumped at the woman's voice. He and Damon both leapt to their feet.

A slim blonde woman sat on his baby grand.

"Who the hell are you?" Damon demanded.

She slid off the piano and walked over to the couch. She wore dark pants and a white shirt unbuttoned enough that Marco thought he could see the lace of her bra.

"You were just talking about me," she said.

"We were?" Marco asked.

The blonde sat on the back of the couch, running her fingers over the leather. Her straight, silky-looking hair swung gently around her face.

"The Grand Master sent you?" Damon asked.

"Yes."

"Do we get to know your name?" Marco asked. Despite the seriousness of the situation, he was captivated by the blonde. Her skin was pale and creamy, her cheekbones high and pronounced. He was struck by a desire to have her look at him so he could see what color her eyes were.

"I'm Tasha."

"Tasha who?" Damon demanded.

She focused on Damon. They stared at each other for a long moment. Marco raised one brow—it was a brave soul who would attempt to stare down Damon Corzo.

"You do not need to know more than that. Show me the video."

"Not until we have some proof about who you are."

She sighed and then started unbuttoning the bottom of her shirt.

"Well, this is interesting." Marco sat down, crossed his legs and prepared to enjoy the show.

She opened her shirt enough to expose the top of her pants and her flat belly. She wore a gold belly chain and dangling from it was a small tri-spiral pendant. It was the sign of the Trinity Masters—a match to the large signet rings he and Damon both wore. "Enough?" she asked.

"Fine." Damon set down his drink, went to his bag and pulled out his tablet.

The blonde's focus shifted to Marco. Her eyes were blue—a pale clear blue with a ring of darker color around the outside. She was strikingly beautiful—the kind of beauty that spoke of strength and sexuality.

"Why do you wear it there?" he asked her.

"Identifying jewelry is dangerous. When I have to wear it I make sure no one can see it, that no one knows I have it on."

"I wouldn't have said it was dangerous, but then again we're being blackmailed because our rings might give us away." Marco smiled at Tasha, but she didn't react.

"Here." Damon handed her his tablet.

She tapped the screen. The buzz of video background noise filled the living room.

"Come here, baby," a female voice said.

"You think you can handle both of us?" Damon's voice was nearly unrecognizable—he always got growly when he was having sex.

"Need me to fuck you harder?" Marco winced as he heard

his own voice. He'd been deep in the pretty redhead's pussy when she beckoned Damon over.

"*Oh yeah, fuck me harder while surfer-boy fucks my mouth.*"

Tasha rolled her eyes. "This is uninspired."

"You're critiquing our blackmail video?" Damon asked.

"No. I'm critiquing her performance. It's clear she's setting you up."

"She's hardly the blackmailer," Marco said. "She's not taking the video."

Tasha's gaze swung to him. The video continued to play, the soundtrack now just groans and the slap of flesh. "You think that this woman was not a part of the plan? That she did not purposefully put herself in this position?"

Marco looked at Damon, who was running his hands through his hair. "We didn't...I mean she's hardly the first woman we've shared."

Tasha smiled slightly. "And you just assume no woman can be in the same room as both of you without wanting to fuck you in tandem?"

"Insulting our intelligence isn't helping. If it's your professional opinion that she was part of this blackmail plot then we'll deal with that." Damon's voice was cool and calm, but Marco could hear the frustration he was trying to hide.

Tasha tipped her head to the side, her hair swinging. "Very well. I will do my job and not say anything more about it." There was something in her voice that made Marco sit up. It was almost as if she'd been hurt by Damon's tone.

Damon must have heard it too. "I'm sorry if I misspoke. I simply want this situation resolved. I tried to resign, but the Grand Master wouldn't let me."

"Of course not," Tasha said. "I understand you are valuable

and they have plans for you." She handed the tablet back, rose and walked across the room to the bar.

Marco shrugged when Damon looked at him in confusion. There was something strange about Tasha, some subtext he couldn't figure out. As she added ice and vodka to a shaker, Damon sat on the back of the couch near Marco and leaned over.

"Who do you think she is?" Damon whispered.

"You mean *what* is she?'" Marco watched her back. "I don't know. She's not what I expected."

"She may be some corporate security agent—someone who specializes in finding and deleting information."

"That sounds boring." Marco shook his head at Damon's lack of imagination.

Damon snorted and sat up as Tasha returned to them carrying an iceless glass of clear liquid—chilled vodka, served neat.

"Salute." She raised her glass to them and then downed the contents in one swallow.

"Whoa," Marco muttered.

"Mmm hmm." Damon raised his glass to his face to cover his response. "Cheers." He took a drink and Marco followed suit.

"Now, gentleman, tell me the rest." Tasha brushed past Damon as she made her way around the couch and Marco saw his friend stiffen.

When Damon didn't respond, Marco answered her request. "The party was about a month ago. We were in Vegas. I had a concert—one night only at Caesar's Palace. Damon flew out from L.A. to join me."

"Where were you when this was taken?"

"In my suite."

"And how did you meet the women you were with?"

"Some of them had invitations to the patrons' party. It was after the concert, ten thousand a person for those who wanted to mingle with the artists."

Tasha raised a brow. "Each of these women could afford ten-thousand-dollar tickets to a classical music party?"

"You think beautiful young women won't spend money on the arts?"

"I think beautiful young women don't have to pay to attend parties in Las Vegas."

Damon snorted out a laugh. Marco nodded, conceding the point.

"We went to Pure, the nightclub in Caesar's," Damon said. "It was after the patrons' party closed down at midnight. At least fifteen people from the patrons' party—men and women—went with us. But by the time we left the club at two a.m. the men were gone and we'd acquired a few more women."

Tasha nodded and crossed her legs, drawing attention to the slim columns of her thighs. "And did you invite them all up to your room?"

Marco shrugged. "I don't exactly remember. We'd had a few cocktails."

"Then I'm suitably impressed by your sexual prowess considering you were drunk."

This time it was Marco who laughed. For the first time, a true smile curved Tasha's lips. It was gone as soon as it happened.

"How many women were there?" she asked.

Damon was rubbing his head. "Eight, ten? We didn't have sex with all of them. There was a blonde I was with, and then the redhead we shared."

Tasha's gaze was cool. "You talk about her as if she were a bottle of wine you split."

"I didn't mean...we absolutely respect women." Damon looked grim.

"I'm sure you do. What was her name?"

Marco looked at his friend. Her name?

"Well..." Marco said. "I don't think we know."

"As I said. She was nothing more than a commodity to you—a bottle of wine. Though I suspect you remember the names and vintages of wines more than you remember the names of the women you fuck."

An unfamiliar feeling curdled in Marco's gut. He felt...guilty.

"You think we deserve what happened to us," he said to Tasha.

"No, blackmail is a heinous thing. I have no doubt that the women you've been with were using you just as much as you were using them." Tasha's gaze moved between them. "Together you are quite the pair. Dark—" she motioned to Marco "—and light." She gestured to Damon.

"Well, we've established that we're idiots for bringing women from a club to our hotel, and that we're pigs for fucking them. Now that we're done with the guilt trip, what do we do?" Damon's voice was hard, demanding. He did not like to dwell on anything, either good or bad. He liked solutions.

Marco would have preferred to continue talking, to explore Tasha's words, to understand her censure. It was a novelty having someone comment on his behavior. Their position with the Trinity Masters meant they had been free to indulge themselves, essentially operating outside societal norms. They would be married when they were called to the altar and until then they had no one but themselves to answer to.

At least that had been true until the blackmail.

Tasha rose and crossed to where Marco sat. She knelt on the couch between him and Damon and laid a hand on both of their shoulders. Marco could smell her perfume, see the lace of her bra. She was slim and lithe. Unbidden, an image of her on her knees, that silky hair wrapped around his hands, rose in Marco's mind's eye.

"Tell me the rest," she whispered. "Tell me everything."

The shift from confrontational to confessional had Marco scrambling to make sense of her.

"There's, uh, not much more." Damon sounded as flustered as Marco felt. "A link to the video was sent to my personal email. I tried to trace the account it came from but there was no name. I know a bit about computers and I was able to track the IP address back, but it bounced around, and as far as I can tell it originated in Morocco."

"I'm impressed you were able to do that." Tasha smiled softly and leaned in to Damon. "Is there anything else that happened? Even something small?"

"Someone stole Marco's phone," Damon said, gazing into Tasha's eyes.

"Damon!" Marco barked, reaching past the blonde to smack his friend.

Damon shook himself and then looked at Marco. "Fuck."

Tasha rose to her feet. "I knew you were holding something back when you reported to the Grand Master."

Damon frowned. "You were there?"

"Yes."

"But...where?"

"Sitting in the office."

"What? How did I not see you?"

"Very few people can see me when I don't want to be seen." She was back to being hard and matter of fact.

"Who *are* you?" Damon demanded.

Marco was holding his breath, hoping they wouldn't circle back to the issue of his stolen phone.

Tasha faced him. "What was on your phone?"

Apparently Marco's luck was not that good.

"My contacts, calendar." He shrugged.

"Something more than that, otherwise you wouldn't be hiding the fact it was stolen."

Marco looked at Damon. "I'm sorry," his friend muttered. "She Jedi mind tricked me."

Marco snorted. "You're a disgrace."

"I know."

"Gentlemen." Tasha sat on the coffee table and leaned forward, elbows braced on her crossed knee. "What was on the phone?"

"Photos."

"Of?"

"Of the Winter Gala."

Tasha's eyebrows rose. "The public reception?"

"Some...and some in the private party."

Tasha shook her head. "That is a problem."

Four times a year, the Trinity Masters hosted grand galas in the Boston Library. Half the party took place upstairs and was open to the public—the wealthy public. Potential new members—usually undergrads from the world-class universities in and around Boston—were invited, as were influential people who were not part of the organization. It was an excuse to bring the members of the Trinity Masters together in one place. As the public party wound down, the private party in their secret headquarters under the building started up. Often there was a formal meeting included as part of the event, but Marco rarely attended that—he was there for the festivities. It was a chance to meet other members and indulge himself with people who, like him, could not commit themselves to a relationship because they were waiting to be called to the altar.

"Could other members be identified from the pictures?" she asked.

"I don't think so," Marco answered. "We were all wearing our masks, but there are photos of members upstairs." He hadn't wanted to tell anyone about the phone because he couldn't bear the idea that he'd betrayed the trust of his fellow members. There were few things as important to him as the Trinity Masters. The video was clearly the more pressing threat, and as far as he knew the phone might simply have been lost. He'd had it at some point, but by the next morning it was gone. "It shouldn't be a problem," he told Tasha. "I was able to log into my account and delete the contents of the phone."

"And were you able to trace its location?"

"No, that had been disabled."

"Meaning whoever took it knew enough to prevent you from recovering it."

"Or it fell out of my pocket and was run over by a car on the boulevard."

"That would be very lucky, but I doubt it's the case."

Damon broke in to the conversation. "The probability of someone using the video of us, plus the pictures on Marco's phone, to positively identify the existence of the Trinity Masters is slim. The likelihood of them correctly picking out members from photos or the attendee list of the Winter Gala is so narrow—"

"It is not as improbable as you think. There are things you don't know." Sasha stood. "We have to find these women—the redhead and whoever took the video."

"We?" Marco asked.

"What happens when we find them?" said Damon.

Tasha cocked her head to the side. "You thought I would simply clean up after you? No. You—" she pointed at Marco "—will go with me to Las Vegas." Her attention shifted to Damon.

"And when I find them?" She smiled, and it was not a kind expression. "Perhaps it's best I don't tell you."

She rose to her feet. "Marco, be ready at eight am. A car will pick you up. Damon, you may return to Los Angeles." She nodded once and then left, letting herself out.

Damon looked stunned. Marco felt a bit dazed himself.

Their gazes met. "Holy shit," Damon said.

Marco went to get another drink.

Holy shit indeed.

CHAPTER THREE

Marco leaned on the handle of his suitcase and yawned. It had been a long time since he'd had to get up so early. Most of his work happened at night—be it concerts or composing.

Damon had gone to bed at two a.m., but Marco had been up until four. Worry and frustration over the situation had kept him awake, and the only way to work through the feelings was to play. Luckily, Damon, who was sleeping in the same room he'd used while he'd been living in the condo, had learned to sleep through the sound of Marco's cello.

By the time he went to bed at four, his soul was at peace. However, when his alarm went off at seven he'd felt decidedly un-peaceful. More so because he wasn't able to indulge in his normal routine of coffee, a run and then reading the paper.

A black sedan pulled up to the curb. The driver got out and silently opened the trunk. Marco handed him his bag and opened the rear door.

"Good morning," Tasha said as he slid into the backseat.

"I dislike mornings." Marco leaned his head back and closed his eyes.

"I see that. Luckily, it's a quick flight."

"I hope we're flying first class," he said, not caring that he sounded like a diva.

"We are. I didn't think the famous Marco Polin would agree to coach."

"Famous?" He snorted. He didn't feel famous right now. He felt tried and grumpy.

"Aren't you?"

"Perhaps, among those who enjoy accessible classical music."

"I do." Her words were so quiet he almost didn't hear her. "I saw you play in London. It was transcendent."

Marco sat up, suddenly wide awake. "What was that?"

Tasha was looking out the window. She didn't acknowledge his question.

An hour and a half later they were at O'Hare airport in the first-class airline lounge. Marco had finally gotten his coffee and his paper and was feeling more himself. Tasha sat across from him with a cup of tea and a plate of fruit.

"Why did he send you?" Marco asked as he sipped his coffee.

"Who?"

"The GM." Marco used the shorthand name for the Grand Master since they were in public.

"He must have thought I could help you."

"And why did he think that? What do you do?"

Her lips twitched. "That's classified."

"Do you work for Price at Bennett Securities?"

Tasha frowned. "You know him?

"No. Damon knows he's a member. That's who he thought the GM would send."

"Then I'm sorry to disappoint you."

"I'm not disappointed."

The attendant came by to let them know their flight was boarding. It wasn't until Marco was buckled in beside her that he realized she'd managed to completely avoid his question.

Tasha's blood started humming as the plane touched down. It was a familiar feeling, the calm anticipation before an op. She'd slept a few hours and spent the rest of the night gathering the information she needed. It had been easy enough to run an image of the redhead through facial-recognition software she'd plugged into the Nevada state DMV database.

In a matter of minutes, she had a name and address. If that was all that was needed, she was sure there were dozens of Trinity Masters who could have done what she did. People like Price, who operated within the law, sometimes dipping into gray areas.

Tasha didn't even pretend the things she did were legal, and to take care of a blackmailer she would need to do things many people would not be willing to do. Especially if the Grand Master's fears were correct and there was more to this situation than Marco and Damon knew.

Marco Polin and Damon Corzo. They were not what she'd expected. When the Grand Master had told her about the situation, she'd been prepared for them to be slightly stupid and vulgar. Despite what she'd said to them, she did not find their behavior offensive.

Marco was all dark, tortured artist. His black hair was a bit too long, his jaw shadowed with stubble. He was lean and tall with long fingers and skilled hands. Damon was gold and bronze. She understood why the woman in the video had referred to him as a surfer boy. With his suit on he looked fit, but his naked body, which she'd gotten a good look at in the video, was all hard muscles and gold skin. His hair was light brown, streaked with gold, and his eyes a warm hazel.

Each of them had the kind of presence that demanded and commanded attention. Together that was magnified until they seemed almost larger than life—the dark angel of music and the golden warrior of justice.

Shaking her head at her fanciful musings, Tasha waved her hand, motioning over the middle-aged chauffeur who held up a sign with her name on it.

"That's my bag," she said, pointing.

Marco was beside her and lifted her bag and his own before the chauffeur could.

"I'll take those, sir."

"Thank you."

The driver led them to a nondescript silver compact. He took off his hat and scrubbed a hand through his hair.

"Will this work, Tasha?"

"It's perfect, Omar. Thank you."

With a nod, Omar walked away, stripping off the suit jacket as he went.

Marco watched him go with wide eyes. "What just happened?"

"Get in."

Tasha took the keys off the front wheel, unlocked the trunk and got into the driver's seat. Marco loaded their bags and then climbed in.

"You're a spy," he said. "That was like a scene out of a movie."

"Movies are fiction." She reached into her large purse and pulled out a stretchy one-shouldered top made out of shiny material.

"But I'm right, aren't I? You're a spy."

"I'm not James Bond, if that's what you mean." Tasha unbuttoned her thin cashmere sweater and stripped it off before pulling her brushed cotton blouse off also.

Marco's gaze dropped to her bra, lingering for a moment before he turned to look out the window.

"You'd make a good James Bond," he said, clearing his throat.

"I do enjoy martinis." Tasha put on the clubbing top and then pulled the strap of her bra down, tucking it inside so that her right shoulder was bare.

"I noticed you went for straight vodka."

"You had good vodka. There was no reason to hide the flavor. You can look now."

"You, Tasha, are one hell of a woman."

It was stupid, but his comment made her smile as she folded her clothes and stuffed them into her bag. She switched her designer sunglasses for a cheap pair of white plastic ones and then added big sparkly earrings.

"Where are we staying?" he asked as she navigated them away from the airport.

"We're not staying. We have a flight back to Chicago tonight."

"Oh. Then where are we going?"

"To Sandra James's house."

"And who is that?"

"The redhead."

"You found her?"

"Yes."

"What are we going to do when we get there?"

"Well, I'm going to kill her and then you're going to help me cut her body up into pieces. Then we'll dissolve it in a vat of acid."

Marco sucked in a breath and held himself very still.

Tasha bit her lip but couldn't hold in her laughter.

"Fuck me," he muttered as she started laughing. "I thought you were serious."

"I'm sorry," she said. "Since you think I'm a spy it seemed like the right thing to say."

He blew out a breath. "So what are we going to do?"

"We're going to talk to her."

"I'm excited about that plan. Very excited."

"Compared to murder and an acid bath that does seem better, doesn't it?"

She took the 215 freeway to Henderson, a suburb of Vegas.

"Have you ever done that?" he asked as she navigated the off-ramp.

"What?"

"Dissolved someone in acid?"

Tasha snorted. That was an unnecessarily messy way to get rid of a body, but she wasn't going to tell him that. "I saw it on *Breaking Bad.*"

Marco laughed until she pulled up outside a three-story apartment building.

She parked at the curb and examined the street. There were enough cars that she doubted they'd be noticed. A neighborhood like this housed people who worked in the casinos, meaning that in the early afternoon they were at home or running errands before going to work. There was plenty of traffic and movement to cover their visit.

"Do you think she's home?" Marco asked.

"She's an escort, so probably."

"She's a *what?*"

Tasha's lips twitched. He looked mortally offended. "An escort. A high-class one if that makes you feel better."

"An escort? I don't sleep with escorts."

"It seems that you did."

"Fuck." Marco rubbed his face. "We really were set up, weren't we?"

"I'm afraid so. It's unlikely an off-duty escort just happened to join your party the same night that a blackmail video was taken."

"Do you think that's what she does? Blackmail people who hire her?"

"A quality escort can make more serving clients than with blackmail. Besides, I thought you said you didn't hire her."

"We didn't, I meant...never mind."

"Let's go."

Together they got out of the car. Tasha took a hair tie from her pocket and pulled her hair up into a high ponytail. She then adjusted her expensive jeans, tugging them down just enough that a bit of belly showed between the waistband and the bottom of the shirt. She laced her arm through Marco's, setting her expression to a casual smile. After a moment of stiffness, he adapted, covering her hand with his and smiling down at her.

Tasha's belly fluttered. Taken aback, she looked away from his smiling face. What was wrong with her that she was having this strange uncontrolled reaction to him? She still wasn't sure why she'd brought him. She never took people with her on ops unless she needed them as bait. The words had popped out of her mouth last night before she could stop them.

They took the stairs to the second floor. Tasha tugged on him to keep the pace slow, giving her time to identify where they were going so that to anyone watching it would seem they knew exactly what they were doing.

She let go of Marco and nudged him so that he was standing beside the door, outside the range of the peephole before she knocked on the door to 210.

A sleepy-looking Asian girl with improbably large breasts opened the door.

"Hello?" The girl shrugged a hoodie on over the tank top and boxers she wore, her eyes, still lined with last night's make-up, were wary.

"Hi." Tasha cocked her hip to the side and grinned. "Is Sandra here? I'm her friend Ashley. I know this is so last minute, but she totally said I should drop by next time I was in town, and here I am."

"Oh." The girl relaxed, leaning on the open door. "Sorry, Sandra doesn't live here anymore."

"Shoot." Tasha let her face fall. "Are you serious?"

"Yeah. She moved out about a month ago."

Around the same time the blackmail video was taken. Marco, who was pressed against the wall to the right of the door, stiffened.

"Do you have her new address? I've totally texted her too, but I think she isn't getting my messages. She never responded when I texted her about coming."

"I think she got a new phone. And she moved away to Boston or Chicago, I don't remember which. She peaced out pretty quick."

Tasha's fingertips were tingling—the woman in the blackmail video all of a sudden moved to Chicago, where Marco lived, or Boston, the headquarters of the Trinity Masters?

"Seriously?" Tasha pouted. "Well, do you have the number for her friend? You know, the super pretty one she always hung out with? I forget her name, but we partied together a couple times. Since I'm in town I totally want to connect with someone local, you know? Go out to the good spots." Tasha kept her smile in place.

"Jennie? Yeah, I have her number. Let me get my phone."

The girl wandered away, leaving the door open. Tasha

stuck her head in and looked around. It was a good-sized place with nice furnishings. Nothing too classy, but the pieces were clearly real wood rather than pasteboard. It wasn't the place a seriously successful escort would live, but Sandra had been working for a service, meaning she wasn't quite at the level of having a private client list and therefore keeping all her profits.

The girl came back, phone in hand. Tasha took her own phone out of her purse and typed in the phone number.

"If Jennie isn't around maybe we could go out?" Tasha smiled, biting her lip as if she were nervous about asking.

"I'm working tonight, but if you come by the club I'll put your name on the list. I'm Jacki, just tell them you're with me." Jacki reached over and grabbed a card off the entry table. "I work at the club at Caesar's."

"Pure, right?" Tasha said. "That's so cool. I've heard it's a sick scene."

"It can get intense. I'll hook you up."

"Thank you so much. I'm gonna call Jennie, and then I'm totally going to see you tonight."

Tasha hugged Jacki, taking advantage of the instant friendship girls were able to create, then with more promises of seeing her later, Tasha walked away.

Marco remained pressed to the wall until the door closed. Tasha held up her hand, motioning for him to wait for thirty seconds before he joined her by the stairs.

"Chicago or Boston?" he said as they made their way to the car.

"An interesting coincidence, don't you think?"

"The situation was bad, but it feels like it's getting worse."

They got into the car and Tasha pulled up her phone. She plugged the number Jacki had given her into a tracer program and got a name and address.

"Guinevere Mallory. She lives not far from here," Tasha reported.

"Guinevere? Jennie?"

"If my name were Guinevere I'd use a nickname too."

"And you think she's the one who took the video?"

"Whoever Guinevere/Jennie is, she's important enough to Sandra that she was the first person Sandra's former roommate thought of when I asked for her friend."

Tasha tapped in the address and started the car.

CHAPTER FOUR

Tasha drove past the address she'd gotten for Jennie. A block later, she pulled into the parking lot of a liquor store.

"Was that it?" Marco asked. "It didn't look like an apartment."

"It wasn't." Tasha checked her phone again. "It's a fetish club."

Marco's eyebrows rose. "It's a what?"

"I thought maybe the club was on the first floor of a condo building, but clearly there's no living space above. That means she gave her work address when she got the phone."

"So the first girl is an escort and this one is a...stripper?"

"More likely she's a fetish model, but there's only one way to find out."

Tasha got out, grabbed their bags from the trunk and threw them into the backseat.

"What are you doing?" Marco asked, twisting to watch as she climbed in with the bags and unzipped her suitcase.

"What else do you have to wear?"

Marco looked down at his slacks and polo. "Pants, shirts."

Tasha rolled her eyes. "That's descriptive."

"What are you looking for?"

Tasha took out a pair of designer leggings. They had panels of leather on the inner thigh and outer calf. Bracing her shoulders on the backseat, she unfastened her jeans and wiggled out of them.

Marco whipped around to face front.

"You seem like the kind of guy who would look." Tasha kicked her pants and shoes off and then tugged on the leggings.

"Normally I would."

"Then why aren't you now?"

"Because..." His voice trailed off.

"Because I'm the one who's cleaning up your mess, or because I'm a member of Trinity Masters and you have to treat me with at least as much respect as a bottle of wine?"

"You don't think much of Damon or me, do you?"

Tasha winced at his half-hurt, half-disgruntled tone but didn't say anything.

"I think it would be worse if I started relationships with people I have no future with because someday I'll be called to the altar." Marco's words were quiet and more sincere than she expected. "I always make it clear to my lovers that I'm looking for a night or two of pleasure, nothing more. Plenty of women have turned me down because that wasn't what they wanted."

I'll be called to the altar.

Tasha stuffed her jeans into her suitcase. Marco was right, it would be cruel of him to start relationships that would never go anywhere. He and Damon and all the other members of the Trinity Masters would eventually be married. Tasha would not. She'd accepted that fact several years ago, around the time the Grand Master had stopped apologizing every time he sent her out on an op.

She took off the silver shirt, slid her bra strap back in place and then put on a tunic-like top made of sheer black material. Her upper body was clearly visible, but the cut of the shirt was ostensibly modest. She closed up her suitcase and started digging through Marco's, selecting items and passing them up to him without a word.

She started running through the scenarios for the op. She'd done hundreds of different ops before her CIA handler had helped to get her off Uncle Sam's radar and into the Trinity Masters. At the age of twenty three she'd already been an agent for the US government for ten years. She'd been so tired and burned out that she'd gotten sloppy—it would have been only a matter of time before she was killed if she hadn't gotten out.

Those first few years had been quiet and peaceful—until the day she'd been summoned by the Grand Master.

She'd gotten her hair done and had a bikini wax, sure she was being called to the altar. Having never had a normal relationship, she was desperately looking forward to her marriage. To outsiders, a trinity union would seem impossibly strange, but to Tasha it had seemed like the answer to a prayer—if there were two other people in the relationship there would be less pressure on her.

But the Grand Master hadn't matched her. He'd needed her to get the CFO of a manufacturing conglomerate to retire. The Trinity Masters had someone in place to take the job, and they needed their person in a position of power before another member formally announced a new plastics recycling process they'd developed.

On the Grand Master's orders, Tasha had seduced the CFO. Not slept with him, but seduced him nonetheless—showing him what life after retirement would be like. Implying that if he did retire he would have the time and the money for an affair with someone like her.

It had taken less than two weeks for her to get him to hand in his letter of resignation. She'd continued the relationship until he formally stepped down.

A few more assignments like that and she'd finally realized she was never going to be called to the altar. The members of the Trinity Masters were some of the smartest and most powerful people in the country. They wanted and deserved elegant partners who elevated them—not a woman who could, and would, seduce a sixty-five-year-old man or break in to a bank.

Tasha thought she'd escaped her former life, but all she'd done was trade one master for another. That had been hard for her to accept, but she finally had, knowing that she would never be deserving of a trinity of her own. At least she was unlikely to be killed or imprisoned doing these jobs.

With some difficulty Marco shed his slacks and pulled on jeans. She watched the muscles of his thighs flex as he lifted his ass off the seat.

When he stripped off his shirt, Tasha had to look away. Something about Marco affected her in a way she didn't understand. It wasn't as if she hadn't seen beautiful men naked before.

"What's the plan?" he asked when he was dressed.

"Get out."

Tasha went to the passenger side and examined Marco head to toe. The slim jeans were okay, but the shirt was clearly meant to go with the black one-button suit he had in his bag. It was starched and pressed.

She grabbed the hem and crushed it in her hands.

"What are you doing?" Marco asked.

"You look like you just took off a tie."

Tasha unbuttoned the cuffs and rolled them up, then she ran her hands up his chest, wrinkling the fabric. She tried to ignore the way he felt below the fabric—warm and firm. She jerked her hands back, rubbed them on her thighs and then ran into the liquor store. She kept her head down and used cash to buy a pair of cheap sunglasses. She ripped the tag off and handed them to Marco.

"Let's go."

"What's the plan?" Marco repeated.

"Not sure." Tasha slid into the driver's seat and drove them to the club. The building was nondescript gray in the afternoon light. Tasha got out and motioned for Marco to follow. They went around to the side of the building where she found an entrance marked staff. Before she rang the bell, she took her hair down and unbuttoned Marco's shirt halfway down his chest.

"Follow my lead. The less you say the more people will fill in the gaps for themselves," she whispered. Marco nodded, his gaze searching her face.

The door opened, metal hinges creaking.

"Yeah?" The man who stood in the doorway was middle-aged and fat. He looked like a rumpled accountant. A stack of mail was under his arm.

"Are you Nero?" Tasha asked, getting the name from the mail he held.

"And who are you?"

"I heard you might be looking for someone."

Nero rubbed the top of his balding head. "I have audition days, you should come back then."

"I'm here now." Tasha scooped a hand through her hair, dipped her chin and looked up at him through her lashes.

Nero examined her head to toe—there was nothing sexual in the way he did it, which was unexpected and a little unnerving. "Okay, come in."

Tasha and Marco followed Nero through the door into a

dark hall. There were doors to a stockroom, the bathrooms and an unlabeled one that they headed for. She could see a section of the club at the end of the hallway. The house lights were on and a uniformed crew was cleaning the dance floor and raised dancers' platforms. The unmarked door led to a good-sized office.

"Sammy, these two just showed up."

Another man sat at one of the two desks in the office. He was clearly related to Nero, though he was younger and had hard, dark eyes.

Sammy looked Tasha over, eyes narrowing as he examined her. His gaze was definitely sexual.

"We don't take guys." Sammy waved at Marco.

"He's my boyfriend," Tasha said. "He's just coming with me to make sure nothing bad happens."

"That's a good idea," Nero said absently as he sat at his desk and started sorting mail.

Sammy snorted. "If he doesn't want anything to happen to you then maybe he shouldn't let you be a stripper."

"This is a strip club?" Tasha sneered slightly. "I thought it was somethin' else. Sorry."

"Wait a sec, blondie. If you're looking for better money than glitter and titty tassels then you're in the right place."

"Cool. I'm Ashley."

"I'm Sammy. Me and my brother own this place." Sammy swiveled his chair, leaned back and crossed his arms. "Strip down and let me have a look."

Tasha heard Marco take a step forward. She tossed a smile over her shoulder. "It's okay, baby, this is how they do it."

The dark glasses obscured his eyes, but she could tell from the way his head moved that he was looking between her and the men. Tasha willed him to go along with it—struggling to ignore the unfamiliar feeling in her belly. She wasn't used to having someone with her, wasn't used to someone objecting to her doing whatever she had to do. Marco nodded once, folding his arms. He wasn't relaxed—she could see the muscle in his jaw flexing, but for now he was playing along.

Tasha stripped out of her leggings, slowly peeling them off and turning as she did it so they got a good view of her ass. Next she pulled off her top, letting it slide slowly down her arm before dropping it to the floor.

Sammy rocked in his chair, nodding. "You've got a nice body. You done kinky before?"

"Yeah, I know how to be a good girl."

Nero chuckled and Sammy reached into a drawer and tossed her a pair of handcuffs. "Put them on."

Tasha locked her hands together in front of her and held out her wrists. "How do I look now?"

"Good." Sammy leaned forward, grabbed the chain connecting the cuffs and yanked.

Tasha was pulled off-balance. Rather than catch herself, she let herself hit the floor, falling hard on her knees. Bowing her head, she held up her wrists like an offering.

"What the fuck are you doing?" Marco growled.

His tone made her shiver, but she raised her voice and said, "It's okay, baby. He just had to check and make sure that I knew how to be a good girl." She tossed her head and looked at Sammy though her lashes. "Am I a good girl?"

"Oh yeah, Ashley, you are."

Nero looked up from his paperwork. "Have you worked in one of our clubs before?"

"No, but my friend told me about you, said it was the best place."

"We have a very good safety record." Nero looked at Marco. "She'll be completely safe when she's on the floor."

Sammy stroked her cheek. Tasha bit her lower lip.

"Oh yeah, look at that face. I bet you'll make some sexy noises when you get whipped." Sammy kept glancing up at Marco, as if checking to see what he'd get away with doing while her boyfriend was watching.

"Who recommended us to you?" Nero asked.

Tasha raised her cuffed hands, placed them behind her neck and arched her back. "My friend," she whispered, breathing deep. Sammy's gaze was glued to her breasts, which were nicely displayed by her black bra. "Jennie." She mumbled the name, hoping the incomplete answer was vague enough that if Jennie walked in she could say that her *friend* told her about Jennie, or, if Jennie wasn't here, that she could claim Jennie was her friend.

"Oh yeah? Are you from Chicago?" Nero looked up and smiled. "I love the pizza there. How is she doing? I keep meaning to call Demario—he's our manager at our club in the windy city."

"She's good, really likes working there," Tasha said, hoping Marco was controlling his reactions. Another move to Chicago eliminated the possibility of coincidence.

"And why did you move to Sin City?" Sammy asked. He grabbed Tasha's chin and forced her head up.

His grip on her jaw was so tight that she couldn't answer.

"She came with me," Marco growled. "Take your fucking hands off her."

Sammy released her. "Listen, buddy, your girl is a glorified stripper, so if you don't want me inspecting the merchandise then I suggest you marry her and keep her locked up at home."

Before Marco could say anything else, Tasha rolled to her feet and bent over. Making sure her breasts were in his face, she whispered in Sammy's ear. "I'll come back later, alone."

"Yeah, you will," he panted. He pinched her nipple,

squeezing hard enough that Tasha didn't have to feign the gasp of pain. The action was hidden from Marco by her position.

"Nice to meet you, blondie," Sammy said loudly enough that Marco and Nero could hear. He took some keys from the desk and undid the cuffs. Tasha pulled on her clothes, thanked Nero, winked at Sammy and then got out of there.

As soon as the door closed behind them, Marco started swearing. "That fucking son of a bitch. How dare he treat you like that? I should have knocked his fucking teeth in."

"You would be in trouble if you broke your hand." Tasha hadn't thought the moody, sexy musician would have a reaction like this. His anger on her behalf was strangely sweet. "It's fine. I've had much worse."

They were halfway across the parking lot when Marco stopped her. "What does that mean?"

She shrugged. "Exactly what I said. I've done worse and had worse done to me." *Much worse.*

Marco seemed on the verge of saying more, but Tasha didn't have time to wait for him to come to grips with her methods.

"We need to go."

Marco blew out a breath. "Back to Chicago?"

"Exactly."

Damon looked up from the dining table as the door to the condo opened.

"Hello?" he called out, getting to his feet.

"Damon? You're still here?" Marco, wearing jeans and a half-open and wrinkled black dress shirt, tossed his bag into a corner. With his dark hair and stubble he looked rougher than his normal easy polished appearance.

"Why didn't you go to Vegas?" Damon asked. "What happened?"

"We did go." Marco motioned over his shoulder as Tasha appeared. She was wearing what looked like black riding breeches and a sweater.

"That was fast." It was just after eleven. They must have gotten on an early afternoon flight.

"Why are you still here?" Tasha pulled her phone and a small black box that might have been an external hard drive from her purse.

"I took some meetings with people from my old firm since I was in town. I have a flight back to L.A. tomorrow morning."

Marco went to the drawer in the kitchen where he kept menus. The cookware and utensils Damon had bought when he lived here were still in the kitchen somewhere, but Marco never used them.

"Persian or Thai?" Marco asked.

"Persian," Damon replied, attention on Tasha. She'd slid onto one of the stools at the breakfast bar and was staring at her phone. "Is either one of you going to tell me what happened?"

Marco tapped Tasha's shoulder. "What do you want to eat?"

"We ate on the plane."

Marco snorted. "That wasn't food." He tapped his phone, keying in the order.

"Excuse me." Damon cleared his throat. "I need someone to tell me what happened in Vegas."

Marco's lips thinned. He jerked his head towards the hall. Damon's nerves were humming as he followed his friend to the stairs and then up to the master bedroom.

"What?" he demanded when the door closed behind them.

"We found them—sort of. The redhead's name is Sandra. She moved right after the party."

"And?"

"She moved to Chicago."

"She's here? Why? That seems strange."

"Actually, her roommate wasn't sure if it was Chicago or Boston."

"Boston? Fuck." Damon ran a hand through his hair. He didn't want that girl anywhere near the Trinity Masters' headquarters.

"And the other girl, the one who took the video—"

"You found her?"

"Maybe. Tasha got us in to the place where she worked—a fetish club—and they said that she'd moved to Chicago."

"Fuck." Damon sank into one of the club chairs by the window. Marco took a seat on the bed. "They moved here? Are they stalking you or something?"

"I was thinking about this on the plane. The video was sent to you, but then they came to Chicago instead of going to L.A. where you are."

"None of this makes sense. They didn't even ask for that much money."

The million-dollar blackmail demand was a lot—enough that Damon would have needed Marco's help to raise the cash —he was a civil servant after all—but it wasn't unreasonable.

"Maybe it's a coincidence," Damon said, but he knew it wasn't. There was something very bad going on.

"I don't think we have that much luck." Marco rose and went to the closet, taking off his shirt and dropping it into a dry-cleaning bag.

"Why are you dressed like that?" Damon asked. It was totally unimportant, but he needed some time to let the new information sink in.

"I posed as Tasha's boyfriend when we went to the fetish club." Marco jerked open a drawer and took out a polo. "She had to pretend she was interviewing for a job working there."

"What do you mean?"

"I mean that she took off everything but her underwear and got manhandled. This fucker named Sammy made her put on handcuffs and then jerked her around." Marco shrugged on a new shirt. "I hate that she had to go through that because of something we did."

Marco's defense of Tasha was unexpected. "I agree that's unsavory, but I assume she's accustomed to being in difficult situations if she's a corporate security agent."

"She's not a corporate security agent. I think she was a spy. A real spy."

"Like a CIA agent?"

"I don't know, maybe." Marco shrugged. "I don't like that someone else may have to get hurt to fix our problem."

"What makes you think that she's going to get hurt?"

"Fine, not hurt, but she may have to do things—like pretend to be a stripper—to help us."

"I agree that it's not ideal, but I'm also enough of a feminist that if she chooses to use her sexuality that way I'm not going to judge her for it." Damon didn't like the idea of anyone—man or woman—cleaning up his mess, but after the way Tasha had gotten him to blurt out the information about the stolen cell phone, he wasn't going to make the mistake of thinking she was helpless.

"She's not what she seems," Marco said. "She's..."

"What?"

Marco shook his head. "I don't know."

"Let's go. I want to hear what she thinks is going on."

Tasha was applying makeup, using the mirror in the foyer. She'd changed clothes and was now wearing black boots, a pair of tiny skin-tight black shorts and a loose black see-though shirt.

"Tasha?" Marco asked.

When she faced them her eyes were rimmed with dark make-up, making her look dangerous, but her lips were a glossy pink.

"I've reported our progress to the Grand Master," she said.

"Was he pissed?" Damon asked.

"He might have been, had I told him everything." She checked her reflection again, this time pulling her hair up into a loose bun that she secured with two black chopsticks. "He doesn't need to know everything we do, only that we've made preliminary identifications and are pursuing the women."

"Thank you," Damon said.

"Where are you going?" Marco asked.

"To the club. I want to see Jennie."

"I'm going with you," Marco declared.

"No, you're not."

"Yes, I am. After what happened in Vegas I'm not letting you go alone."

"You're going to...protect me?" Tasha looked away, and Damon thought for a moment her face changed, her expression sad or uncertain. He stiffened—was she afraid? Planning to put herself in real danger?

"I'm going too," he said, surprising himself.

Marco raised an eyebrow. "I thought you were too much of a feminist."

"Shut up, asshole."

Tasha crossed her arms, making Damon painfully aware of the fact that he could clearly see her bra and the upper swell of her breasts through the shirt.

"You are not going with me. You will stay here and eat your food."

"We're going with you." Damon stepped up to her. Even with heels, she was shorter than him. He was not above using some body-language intimidation to get what he wanted.

"You're going to go to a fetish club? Unless you have alternate IDs you risk your precious reputation."

Damon smiled. "Luckily, I do have one. You might not think it, due to our current situations, but Marco and I know how to be careful."

Tasha looked between them and then shrugged. "Fine. We need to leave. I'll give you instructions on the way."

CHAPTER FIVE

Tasha bit the inside of her cheek to keep from smiling as she looked at Damon and Marco.

Marco wore a black suit with gray dress shirt—the shirt was open down the chest. An untied black necktie dangled from his collar, hinting that he had no intention of using it as an accessory, but rather was willing to take it off at a moment's notice and use it for bondage. He could as easily have been on his way home from an elegant party or evening at the theater as on his way to a fetish club.

Damon she hadn't been as kind to. Once she agreed to let them come, she'd run through Marco's enviably large closet on the second floor master and picked outfits for each man. The easiest way to gain entry to a place was to look the part—that was true of life, not just clubs. Damon could have dressed similarly to Marco, but Tasha wanted to see the aggressive lawyer off-balance. While Marco seemed comfortable in his skin, adapting with relative ease, Damon was like a controlled explosion—each careful word and aggressive action an attempt to impose himself on the world.

Marco stretched his legs out, the limo she'd called giving him the space to do so. "You look good, Damon. I'm going to send a picture to your office."

"Shut up, asshole," he mumbled.

Damon wore leather pants that she'd found in the back of Marco's closet. Nothing but black leather pants. According to the musician, they were from a photo shoot he'd done for one of his albums, where he'd been dressed like a biker while playing the cello. Tasha didn't admit she knew exactly which album he was talking about—the liner notes, which included photos of Marco shirtless with a tattoo of music notes across his back, and another of him with his eyes closed, his face streaked by grease as he cradled the neck of his cello—had caused her to have more than a few fantasies.

Damon's bare upper body showed off skin that was golden where Marco's was pale, his muscles hard swells under that bronzed flesh. Tasha had used some black stage make-up she always carried to add dark streaks to his hair.

The limo pulled to a stop.

"I'll be right back," she said, sliding out. The driver was someone she'd worked with before and knew better than to turn off the car while she ran in to the adult store.

At this time of night, it was mostly men perusing porn DVDs and fleshlights, though this was one of the best sex shops in the city and carried only a limited supply of cheap porn. Tasha ignored their come-ons and grabbed what she needed, plus a few extras.

Ten minutes later, she was back in the limo. Marco and Damon both watched her attentively as she dropped into a seat.

"What did you get?" Marco asked. "I didn't know this place existed." He was peering curiously out the window.

"Masks for you." She pulled out the shaped leather half-masks and passed them out. "You won't be able to put them on until we're inside, but do it as soon as we're in."

Next she took out a leather motorcycle vest. It had cost nearly five hundred dollars, but the large circular symbol on the back made it worth it. She handed it to Damon. It would have been fun to make him go in half naked, but his discomfort might give them away. Better to give him more clothes and make sure the op was a success.

"What's this?" He was holding it up, examining the back.

"That's the symbol for the BDSM community."

Damon sighed, then nodded and slipped it on. Tasha eyed him—with the leather vest on and his muscled arms crossed over his chest, he looked dangerous and not at all lawyerly. He looked like the kind of man that would, and could, do serious damage in a fight as well as in the bedroom.

"You look different." Marco said. "You look like a thug."

"You look like a gigolo."

Tasha smiled to herself, enjoying their easy banter. It was clear the men loved each other. She doubted they'd classify it that way, but Tasha knew how powerful a loving relationship between two people could be—whether those people were lovers, family or friends. It was both the hardest and easiest of relationships to manipulate.

Tasha took out the items she'd bought for herself and ripped off the tags. She slid the cuffs around her wrists and buckled them into place but didn't connect then together with the clip that now dangled from her right wrist. They weren't the subtle, simple kinds that might be mistaken for jewelry. She'd gone for the heavy reinforced-leather and metal ones that were padded on the inside and closed with four separate buckles. They weighed nearly three pounds each.

As she lifted the collar to her neck Tasha was suddenly aware of their attention on her. She looked up.

Damon and Marco were both leaning forward, their focus unnerving.

Tasha put the collar on. Holding it in place with one hand, she slid onto her knees in front of Marco and bent her head, exposing the back of her neck. "Will you fasten it?" she asked quietly.

His fingers brushed her skin. "Tasha, I don't want you to get hurt."

"This will be simple." She knew better than to promise him she wouldn't get hurt. Kneeling like this was making her aware of the bruises that were forming on her knees from falling in Vegas.

"You shouldn't have to do this." Marco took the collar and tossed it onto the seat beside Damon.

Tasha sat back and tried not to get irritated. "I shouldn't have let you come."

"There's got to be another way to get information. We can wait until the morning and go to Jennie's house. You found Sandra's address, you can find hers."

Tasha didn't have time to explain that a place like a club—designed to strip away inhibitions—was much better for gathering information than someone's residence, where they would be more cautious.

She looked at Damon. His jaw was set, his expression shuttered. Tasha shifted to kneel in front of him. She didn't say anything.

Damon picked up the collar, slid it around her neck and locked it in place.

"Damon, what the hell?"

"She knows what she's doing. I'm not going to insult her intelligence by assuming she needs my protection or advice." Though he was speaking to Marco, Damon was looking at her.

Tasha blinked as she sat back. Before she could stop it, she smiled. "Thank you." Even experienced intelligence agents had sometimes looked down on her when she used her gender or age to get information. Damon's trust and respect felt good. It made no sense that she liked both Marco's protectiveness and Damon's respect for her abilities, but she did.

Tasha took the keys to the collar, looped them through pieces of black leather and handed one to each man. Damon slipped his over his head while Marco tucked his into his pocket.

"Close your eyes," she said, going back to her seat. Marco did as she asked. Damon waited until she'd pulled the leather bikini top out of the bag. Once he realized she was stripping to replace her lace bra with black leather, he closed his eyes.

Tasha suspected they were both peeking.

The limo pulled to a stop as she put her shirt back on and stuffed everything into a bag.

"My name is Ashley," she told them. "If you're asked, you're Doms or Masters. I'll refer to you as Sir or Master, depending on what the situation needs." She handed each of them a chain leash. "Keep these with you, playing with them will give you something to do with your hands, but don't agree to play with anyone in there. Don't give anyone your names. If someone asks, ignore them, they shouldn't be asking. Avoid speaking if you can. I'll do the talking for you. If either of you recognizes anyone tug your right ear." Tasha should have spent less time thinking and more time giving them instructions on the way over. She'd just have to hope they could do this.

"Don't we need wires or cellphone videos or something?" Marco asked.

"None of that would be admissible in court." Damon was looking out the window at the front of the club.

"Court? The legal system doesn't exist right now." Tasha

tucked her ID and a few hundred dollars into the waistband of her tight shorts and then got out. "Coming?"

The men shared a look and then followed her out of the limo.

MARCO WAS GRINNING. He couldn't help himself—this was fun.

Due to his relative fame and Damon's need for privacy, their sexual exploits usually took place at a party Marco hosted. Going out like this wasn't an option. They were fine clubbing, but nothing overt could happen in public.

Safe behind his mask, he was able to take in everything that was going on. He'd considered himself jaded and had even occasionally played with some bondage, but nothing near what was represented here. His eyes were being opened to a whole new level of kink.

The inside of the club, which as far as he could tell didn't even have a name, was lit with alternative cool-blue and warm-gold lights. A circular stage in the center of the dance floor sported a large structure shaped like an X. A woman with a shaved head and plenty of piercings was strapped to it. She wore a thong and black tape over her nipples. A man wearing dark jeans and a leather harness circled her, a long whip in his hand. He'd occasionally flick his wrist, the thumping whip against her belly and legs. One wall was glass, and on the other side of it were three gold-lit rooms that reminded Marco of the red-light district in Amsterdam. In one of the rooms, a woman in pink lingerie dangled from the ceiling, her body cradled in a net of ropes. In the next, a girl in retro-style panties and a polka dot bra straddled a two by four, her calf and arm muscles straining to keep her body weight off her pussy. In the third, a woman wearing cat ears, a leopard-print teddy and mitts turned in a circle, showing off her tail.

"Damn," Damon muttered.

"I agree."

"Shh," Tasha whispered to them. "I'm going to the bar to see if I can talk to Demario."

"I'll get us a table," Marco said.

"Then I'll go with Tas—Ashley and get drinks," Damon added.

Marco found a small table in a dark corner. There was a stage behind him, but it was unoccupied. Positioning himself so he could see everything, he settled in to keep an eye on the room. The consternation he'd felt in the limo was gone, replaced by excitement at the novelty of the club.

DAMON SCANNED THE WOMEN, looking for a familiar face. He had only a vague memory of the blonde woman he'd slept with, who he now suspected had taken the video, but he was hoping he'd feel a jolt of recognition.

He accompanied Tasha to the bar, which had a crowd three deep. As they pressed closer, Damon put his hand on Tasha's back in an instinctive gesture. She leaned into him and then nudged his arm farther up her body. Reminding himself of where they were, Damon grabbed her neck and slid his fingers under the back of her collar.

"What can I get you?" the bartender asked, looking at Damon.

"I serve my Master," Tasha said before Damon could reply. "He would like two Glenlivets."

The bartender nodded once and started pouring single-malt scotch. Damon wondered if there was code to the ordering. He wasn't a scotch drinker, but Tasha had rattled off the order as if she'd done it a million times before.

"Is Demario available?" she said.

"Who's asking?"

"Nero and Sammy suggested we might offer him my services."

If Damon hadn't known for sure that the woman he held was Tasha, he wouldn't have recognized her. Her tone was sweet and somehow vulnerable. Her shoulders were soft and relaxed, her body seemingly ready to sway and bend at the slightest order or demand.

The bartender slid the drinks across the bar. Tasha held up a hundred dollar bill and looked at Damon. He raised a brow in question, realizing too late that the mask would hide his expression. Tasha nodded once as if he'd given her some signal and then said, "Yes, Master," and added a second hundred dollar bill. She passed them to the bartender.

"Thank you, sir." He nodded once to Damon.

Taking one of the drinks, he kept his other hand on Tasha. He liked touching her, and some primal part of him liked this feeling of ownership over her. He knew it wasn't real, but still, it was fun playing the silent man who communicated only through his lovely servant girl.

They found Marco, who raised his brow when he saw how Damon was holding Tasha. Damon took a seat as Tasha handed Marco his glass.

"I feel like a Bond villain," Damon muttered.

Marco snorted out a laugh, and Tasha's lips twitched. It was good to see her smile. Damon was rapidly coming to understand Marco's attitude towards the blonde.

"You aren't taking this very seriously." She shifted the table back, clearing floor space between their chairs.

"I'm sorry," Damon said, feeling guilty. "I assure you we haven't forgotten the gravity of the situation."

Tasha bit her lip and met his gaze. "Don't stop. It's...nice." Her brows drew together in confusion, as if she hadn't understood what she was saying.

Before he could say anything else Tasha dropped to her knees between their chairs. She spread her hands on her thighs and bowed her head.

Holding his glass in front of his mouth so no one could read his lips—and feeling like a secret agent as he did it—Damon asked, "What do we do now?"

"Wait and watch," Tasha breathed.

Damon raised his glass.

Marco did the same. "To watching."

Damon rolled his eyes but then went back to scanning the club, hoping that they'd find the girl who took the video and this would all end tonight.

TASHA'S KNEES HURT. The bruises from earlier were making themselves known, but she couldn't exactly get up and take a seat in a chair. Tasha had gone through submissive training at a club in Istanbul when she was seventeen, studied with a professional dominatrix, a famous porn star and a sex therapist. She'd been sold at auction in Beruit, played the *little girl* to a man who wanted to be called *Daddy*, and been the Mistress of a whorehouse in Albania. She knew how to make a man lick her shoes clean and how to take a whipping.

Compared to those places, this club was Disneyland. It was open to the public and had no house rules for submissives, no formal gameplay. There were people of all shapes and sizes, and she saw at least seven distinct sub-kinks represented. Still, she didn't get up, didn't rise from her submissive position. Right now, she didn't want to blend in, she wanted to stand out, to be the submissive everyone was talking about.

The longer they sat there the closer the crowd inched in. A quick look out of the corner of her eye explained why no one had actually come to talk to them. Damon looked like he would break the arm of anyone who dared disturb him. The vest had fallen open, and the key to her collar was clearly visible against his chest. He'd wrapped the chain leash around his fist, as if he were preparing for a fight.

Marco was more relaxed, one leg crossed over the other, but he radiated control. They were sitting in shadow, and the masks hid most of their faces. Tasha wouldn't be surprised if people thought they were the owners of the club, or in some other way figures of authority.

After an hour and a half, Tasha's patience wore out. The club closed at two, and it was nearly one now. She didn't want to come back tomorrow—it was unlikely she was a step ahead of whomever was pulling the strings of this situation, but the faster she moved, the more likely she was to catch up with them before they could cover their tracks.

Kneeling up, she faced Damon and winked. His eyes were burnt gold in the shadows of the mask.

"Yes, Master," she said, just loud enough to be heard. She stripped her shirt off, leaving her naked save the tiny leather bra and shorts. Staying up on her knees, she tucked her wrists behind her neck. This position raised her breasts and stretched out the line of her body.

She felt Marco and Damon's tension notch up, and then fingers touched her back, a gentle caress that was almost like reassurance.

Five minutes later, a man in black pants and a white polo

that was out of sync with the rest of the attire in the club approached them.

"I heard you were looking for me?" the man said.

Tasha raised her head but kept her gaze lowered, staring at his slightly pudgy belly.

"Sir, if you'll allow me, my Master chooses not to speak."

Tasha felt Demario's gaze run over her. "Fine, girl. What does your Master have to say?"

"We've only recently moved here, and at the recommendation of Misters Nero and Sammy we've come to visit you." She spoke slowly and with the overly exaggerated sentence structure that leant an air of rehearsed formality to the words.

"All three of you?"

"No, Sir. My master wears the key to my collar. The other is a new acquaintance who hopes to see you grant my Master's request."

"And what is that request?"

"My Master would like to see me submitting here."

"I see. And you worked for Nero?"

"No, Sir, but I was given the opportunity to fulfill my Master's desires in their club."

She heard Demario sigh. "Hang on." He walked away.

Damon leaned forward to whisper in her ear. "What are you doing?"

"He'll try to verify our story by bringing Jennie out. Right now he doesn't know if we're important or not. He can't risk offending you until he knows."

"Jennie won't recognize you, but she might recognize me or Marco," he whispered urgently. "Then we're fucked."

"First, you need to see if you remember her from that night. Second, you're wearing a mask. If she figures out who you are that might push her into doing something. If she doesn't realize who you are then we have the opportunity to get information from her."

Demario returned. This time Tasha looked up. Demario was younger than Nero or Sammy, and if Tasha had to guess she'd say he didn't find any of this appealing. He looked about as engaged as a warehouse manager.

"Jennie, do you know these two?" he pointed at Tasha and Damon. The woman with him was the tattooed and pierced girl who'd been on the St. Andrew's cross when they walked in.

There was no way this woman would have blended into a crowd at Marco's party. They would have remembered her and been able to describe her.

"Who?" Jennie's face was strangely blank. Tasha examined the other woman, who was naked except for panties and some electrical tape. There was a tattoo of a tree on the inside of her left arm. With a snap, Tasha put it together—this may be the right girl after all.

"Jennie?" she said, smiling a little. "Is that you? You shaved your head. Your hair was so pretty."

Jennie ran her hands over her scalp. "Yeah, yeah I did. He wanted it that way."

Tasha nodded slowly. "I'm sorry for implying you should not have done that. A Master's wishes are the most important thing."

Jennie nodded slowly. "Gotta do what they want so they'll give you what you need." She blinked and looked up at one of the lights. "Can't be gold anymore."

Demario looked disgusted. "Jesus, Jennie. You sound fucking dumb. If that guy didn't drop five large at a time to see you, your ass would be out on the street." His words were low enough that Tasha couldn't hear him, but she could read his lips. She filed everything he said away, seeing the pieces of the puzzle coming together in her mind.

Loud enough to be heard, he said, "Jennie, do you know these two from Vegas?"

"Mr. Nero and Mr. Sammy asked that I say hello when I saw you," Tasha said, making sure it would be hard for Jennie to say no. People hated admitting that they didn't recognize or remember someone. As it was she didn't think Jennie was all there anyway.

Jennie blinked, looking first at Tasha and then at Damon. "Oh yeah, I know them. Big time. These two are hot, super hot."

"Fine. You can go." Demario waved her away.

"Sir, if you please." Tasha leaned toward Marco and cocked her head as if she were listening. He played along and leaned forward, lips pressed to her ear.

"I don't recognize that woman. I don't think it was her," he said.

Tasha nodded. "I will ask for you, Sir." To Demario, she said, "My Master's friend would like to spend some time with Jennie."

"That's up to her. I don't play these weird games." Demario caught himself. "I'm sorry, I didn't mean it like that. I just... It's been a long day."

Marco pointed two fingers at Jennie, crooked them in a come-here gesture and then pointed at the floor at his feet. Jennie's eyes widened and she scrambled to obey. Even Tasha felt a little flutter at that display of casual dominance.

Demario cleared his throat. "Uh, what did your, um, Master, want exactly?"

"As I said, he'd like to have me perform at your club."

"He wants me to give you a job?"

"No, Sir. He simply wants an audience."

Demario stuck his hands in his pockets, took them out again. "We have pretty strict rules about what can happen here. People aren't allowed to just come and play."

"Rules?" Tasha asked.

"No full nudity. No real spankings, whippings, anything like that. If you saw Jennie when you came in, then you saw her getting beat with a fake whip made out of lightweight plastic and velvet. It's all fake, a performance. That's how we're zoned."

Tasha's mind was racing, but she nodded. "We understand, Sir."

"Okay then, yeah, you're welcome to do your thing." Demario looked around. "Would that stage work? I'll get the lights on."

"Yes, thank you."

"What are you drinking? I'll send over a bottle as a thank you for coming in and giving us a bit of a show."

"My Master prefers single-malt scotch."

"Oh, uh, okay. Maybe not a bottle."

When Demario was gone, Tasha rose to her feet and perched on Damon's knee, crossing her arms behind her back. He closed his big, warm hands around her waist, stroked his thumbs over her belly. Tasha doubted he realized he was doing it, but for her it felt as intimate and powerful as if he'd fucked her. She shouldn't be having this reaction to him.

"Marco says he's never seen that woman before," Tasha whispered to him, trying to ignore the way she was shivering in reaction to his touch.

"I didn't think it was her either, but her voice—there's something familiar about it. It's hard to imagine her with hair and without all the piercings, but maybe it is her. She changed a lot. On purpose?"

"Undoubtedly. And I think she's drugged."

"What?"

"The tattoo on her arm. That's to cover track marks. Either she was a druggie before, or they got her addicted after she took the video in order to keep her quiet."

"Who are *they*?"

"Later. We need to talk about what's going to happen next."

"I assume we're leaving."

"No. I need to be alone with Jennie, and I'd like to see the back room or office. Someone is paying big money to visit her—paying enough that Demario is keeping her on staff when he doesn't want to. I need the name of that person."

"So what, I create a distraction and you sneak away?"

"Something like that."

Behind them two spotlights clicked on and illuminated the raised platform set against the wall. It was about eight feet wide, four feet deep and three feet off the floor. Tasha looked from it to Marco and Jennie.

Marco had his hand on the back of Jennie's neck, a mimicry of how Damon had held her. Jennie's eyes were closed and she was swaying slightly. She was high or seriously drunk, possibly both.

"Damon, this will work if you do what I need you to." Tasha met his gaze—this close his eyes were green rimmed in gold.

"What do you need?"

"When we get up on stage you need to use your belt on me."

"Tasha—"

"Give them a show. I want you to do it hard enough that everyone hears it—get everyone in the club looking at us. Fold the belt in half—it will make a lot of noise. Then hit me harder, somewhere unexpected. I'm going to cry like you're really hurting me and try to get away."

His eyes flicked side-to-side as he searched her face. "What's the endgame?"

"When I resist you're going to hit me."

"Keep going with the belt?"

"No, I mean really hit me. In the face."

Damon's whole body jerked. "Absolutely not."

"You do that, I'll fall off the stage into Marco and Jennie. Then I'll get Jennie to take me to the back. The guards and Demario will be busy throwing you out—there will be no one back there."

"I'm not going to beat you with a belt and then punch you."

"Not punch, backhand."

"No. I will *not* do that." His hands squeezed her waist.

A little shiver of happiness worked its way through Tasha. She pushed the useless feeling aside. It was nice to have another protector, but right now she needed someone who would hit her.

"Okay, that's fine. I'm going to invite someone from the crowd onstage with me. All I need you to do is nod as if you ordered me to do it. Then, when they hit me, make a big scene while Jennie takes me into the back."

"Wait, no. I don't want *anyone* to hit you. Me or anyone else."

"I don't have time to argue." She tried to get up but he held her in place on his knee.

"We'll switch," he said, words tinged with frustration. "I'll be the sub, you hit me."

"I think it's a bit late for that plan." It was such a sweet offer that Tasha impulsively leaned forward and kissed his cheek.

She jerked back, moving so fast that he didn't have time to tighten his hold. Tasha dropped to her knees in front of him.

Her heart was pounding in her chest. What was wrong with her? Why had she done that?

He leaned forward. "Are you okay?"

She tried to move away, but he caught her by the ring at the front of her collar. For the first time since she'd put it on it was used for its intended purpose—to control her. It should have made her angry, or helped snap her out of this flustered state, but instead all it did was make her aware of Damon's eyes, his lips, his strength.

"Are you okay?" he repeated.

"Fine. I shouldn't have done that."

"That peck on the cheek?"

The way he said it made it clear that it meant nothing to him. Tasha closed her eyes. *It meant nothing to him.* She held onto that, focusing on it until she had herself under control.

"Do you want me to get someone from the crowd?" she asked him.

He searched her face and then shook his head. "No. I'll do it. Are you sure I have to—"

"Hit me as hard as you can."

"Absolutely not."

"Trust me. I know it's coming, and I can pull away from it. In reality you'll barely have touched me, but it will look bad."

"What if you don't move in time? I box to relieve stress. I could really hurt you."

She winked. "You can try."

That seemed to be what he needed, because he stood, pulling her up by the arm. "Let's do this."

CHAPTER SIX

Marco turned his chair and watched Damon lift Tasha onto the stage. Under the bright lights, her skin seemed pale and delicate. In contrast, Damon looked like a gladiator with his thick muscles and gold skin. The mask and darkened hair added to the impression that the man up there was someone Marco didn't really know.

He'd kept his hand on Jennie's neck once she'd repositioned herself. There was something wrong with her—he could only assume she was drunk, though if she was working that seemed a bit strange. He didn't know what Tasha's plan was, but it was clear she wanted him to keep an eye on Jennie.

People were crowding around, whispering and wondering about what was going on. That was a good question, and Marco wished he knew the answer. Jennie wasn't who they were looking for—she hadn't been at the party. He would have remembered a girl who had piercings in her eyebrows, nose, lips and cheeks—not to mention the shaved head.

And yet Damon and Tasha were planning something—clearly this wasn't the dead end Marco thought it was.

He settled back in his chair, curious and a little excited to see what Damon and Tasha were about to do. He loved seeing his friend like this—stripped of the grim legal shell he wore while at work. Normally, it took a whole weekend of partying to get the real Damon to appear, but now not only was the veil of refinement gone, but he seemed more raw and brutal than Marco had ever seen him before.

Tasha turned her back to the crowd, spread her legs and raised her arms above her head. Her body was smooth and taut, almost completely displayed due to the brevity of what she wore.

Damon's mouth was set in a firm line as he looked out over the crowd. The mask covered his face from hairline to midcheek, and the angle of the lights meant that his eyes were hidden in shadow.

Behind Marco, the crowd quieted, and someone turned down the music. Everyone was waiting with a collectively held breath. Damon ran one finger down Tasha's back. She whimpered, and it was the sexiest sound Marco had ever heard. From the rumbles coming from the crowd, it seemed other people thought and felt the same.

Damon unwound the metal leash from his hand and attached it to the lock at the back of the collar. It dangled down Tasha's back, bumping gently against her tight ass. Damon unbuckled his belt and slowly drew it from the loops of the pants.

Marco sat up, his hand falling away from Jennie. Were they really going to do this?

Damon folded the belt in half. Circling Tasha, he traced patterns on her skin with the leather. Watching them together aroused Marco in a visceral way that he hadn't experienced in a long time. He wanted to see Damon fucking her, wanted to watch them together…then join them.

Damon positioned himself beside Tasha, raised his arm and struck.

The crack of the leather was loud and startling. Tasha moaned and arched her back. Damon struck again, belt cracking against her ass.

Marco found himself counting. At ten, Damon paused and rubbed Tasha's butt. She was moaning and whimpering continuously, and with each strike she moved a bit—shifting her weight, wiggling around.

Damon grabbed her hair, jerked her head back.

Tasha gasped. "Please, Master." She looked up into Damon's face. Releasing her hair, Damon took the leash and pressed it into her mouth, forcing her to hold it between her teeth.

Marco saw Tasha's eyes widen, saw a shiver make its way down her back. He frowned—he'd assumed they'd planned all of this. Assumed that her wiggles and pants were acting, but that reaction seemed real.

Damon took his position beside her and raised the belt. This time the leather slashed against her upper back. Tasha screamed and stumbled forward. Marco's fingers closed around the arms of the chair, but he held still, not wanting to ruin whatever they were doing.

Behind him people muttered. Someone whispered, "That's right, whore, take it."

It was all Marco could do not to find the speaker and beat them black and blue.

"Back in position," Damon growled. He grabbed the dangling leash, which had dropped from her mouth and jerked Tasha forward.

"No, Master!" She held up her hands and pushed against him.

Damon let go of the leash, raised his right arm across his body and viciously backhanded her.

Marco was out of his chair as the sound of the slap died. He was ready to jump up onstage and separate them—and then figure out what the *hell* had gotten in to Damon—but Tasha stumbled from the force of the blow and fell off the platform into Marco's arms.

"I've got you," he whispered.

"Put me with Jennie," Tasha demanded. "Then stay with Damon. The limo is at The Bean."

Marco had only a moment to take in the fact that Tasha didn't seem shocked or frightened, meaning the slap was planned. He guided her to where Jennie knelt. Tasha let out a loud sob then curled against the other woman. Jennie was blinking rapidly but wrapped her arms around Tasha.

Marco turned back to Damon, who'd folded his arms across his chest and was staring out at the crowd. As Demario and a bouncer rushed up to the stage, yelling at Damon, Marco looked over his shoulder to see that Tasha and Jennie were gone.

Tasha took the needle from Jennie's arm. Bending the tip back she wrapped it in a paper towel and put it in the trash.

As soon as they'd gotten away from the crowd, Tasha had asked Jennie for something to help with the pain. The woman's eyes had lit up and she'd pulled out a bottle.

Tasha took the bottle from the mirror, which was lying on the seat of a chair. A powdery white residue from the crushed pills remained.

Diamorphine.

Shaking her head, Tasha wiped the bottle with a paper

towel to clear her fingerprints and then put it back. Diamorphine was prescription heroin, and far more dangerous than the street grade stuff, which wasn't pure. Though these were pills that she could have swallowed, Jennie had crushed, cooked and injected the drug—the mark of a hardcore addict.

Propping her up, Tasha looked around the small office where they were hiding. Jennie had warned her they shouldn't be in here, but the way she wedged the door closed and set up the mirror on the chair said that Jennie had done this plenty of times before.

Tasha went to the computer and opened the bookkeeping software. After only a few minutes she found them—weekly entries of $5,000 each that had started a month ago. They were marked as *private event—Guinevere*, and the payment type was listed as *check*.

Check? Not cash?

Tasha frowned, clicking through until she found the bank-generated scan of the check. It was handwritten. The account name was Trinity and the memo line said, *Hello, Harrison.*

Tasha closed her eyes. This was as bad as it could be.

She opened a ghost email server and pasted and attached the things she wanted into a draft email, then closed it without sending and deleted the browser history. Looking down at Jennie, she picked up the phone and dialed.

"Nine, one, one, what's your emergency?" the calm voice of the operator hummed through the landline.

"Hi, I'm at this club on Taylor St. and there's this girl here who was trying to sell me some pills she said were heroin, and I just found her in the office and I think she's dead." Tasha let out a little sob. "She's on the floor and I can't tell."

"Ma'am, can you check if she's breathing?"

"Wait, yeah, she's...oh my God." Tasha slammed down the phone. She wiped everything free of her fingerprints, opened the office door and followed the hall to an emergency exit. Someone had left a coat hanging on the corner of the lockers near the back door. Bundling herself into it, she got out before anyone saw her.

A block away she heard the wail of fire trucks and ambulances headed for the club.

Glad for the coat, Tasha gathered up the dangling leash and tucked it into her bra strap as she walked toward Sculpture Park and The Cloud Gate, the massive modern art piece locals called The Bean.

"I can't believe I did that." Damon sat on a bench in the dark garden, head in his hands. "I hit her. I've never hit a woman before. I don't hit women. That's not who I am."

"I thought you respected her expertise and were going to do what she said?" Marco was lounging against a tree. The limo idled in a red zone, and they could have waited more comfortably in there, but by unspoken agreement they weren't leaving the park until Tasha showed up.

"I do. That's why I did it. But...fuck." Damon ran his hands through his hair. "Men who hit women deserve to be castrated."

"My friend, you need to calm down. I'll admit I was ready to deck you until I realized it was all part of her plan."

"You know what else was part of her plan?" Damon started pacing.

Marco sighed and took the seat he'd vacated. "No, what?"

"She said she was going to pull away, that I'd barely touch her, but I definitely made contact. *I hit her.*"

"Why are you out here?" Tasha's voice made them both jump. She was standing in the shadows under The Bean.

"Tasha? Are you okay? I'm sorry." Damon started toward her.

Tasha grabbed his arm and hauled him toward the limo.

"Don't say anything else. You shouldn't be out here in the open talking about this."

Damon let her march him to the limo and scrambled in. Marco followed him. Tasha was last in. She went to the front partition and rapped out a pattern.

"Secret knock?" Marco asked.

"Morse code." Going to the built-in bar, Tasha lifted out the ice tray, set it aside and then pulled a cell phone from the interior.

"Tasha, what's going on?" Damon asked.

In the dim lights, he could see her face just enough to make out the concerned expression. Whatever caused Tasha to worry was probably the kind of thing that would make most people cry.

"Hello," she said. "I'm with them."

She huddled against the seat in the too-large coat that covered everything but her long, bare legs.

"It's not an isolated incident. There was a message." She listened and then said, "The girl who took the video is being kept compliant and close to Marco—she's in Chicago. Someone is supplying her with medical grade H and paying to keep her employed at a club. I found the payment records—checks, written from a company called Trinity with a note that says, 'Hello, Harrison.'"

Damon stiffened, looked at his friend and then turned his attention back to Tasha. What did that all mean?

"Fine." She held out the phone to Damon. "He wants to talk to you."

"Fuck," Marco whispered.

Damon took the phone and held it to his ear. "Hello?"

"Mr. Polin." The Grand Master's tone was cool.

"Grand Master." He'd suspected that was who Tasha had called, but it was unnerving to hear his voice.

"What did Tasha do in order to obtain this information?"

"I'm sorry?" The question took him off-guard—that wasn't what he'd expected the Grand Master to ask.

"I assume you were with her."

"Uh, yes. I was, and Marco was with her in Las Vegas."

"She allowed both of you to work with her?"

"Yes. I thought that's what you wanted?"

"It is. What role did she play?"

"She organized it," Damon said, still unclear as to what the Grand Master was asking.

"I mean where did you go and what did you do to obtain the information?"

"She...she pretended to be a submissive. We were in a fetish club. Then she..." Damon fisted his hand on the seat. "Then I hit her—with a belt and then with my fist. We were up on a stage and she asked me to, but I should not have done it. I'm very sorry."

"Enough, Mr. Polin. I have no doubt that you were following Tasha's plan. I simply wanted to understand what she did to get the information."

Damon frowned. "Grand Master, I think a good case could be made that all her actions were justifiable if not technically legal."

"That is the last thing I'm worried about. Please return the phone to Tasha."

She listened for a moment after he passed it back and then said, "I will make it clear that this door is closed and render these pieces and players too expensive to keep in the game."

She hung up the phone, tucked it back into the hidden space and replaced the ice bucket.

"Tasha," Marco said. "What's going on? What's really going on?"

She shook her head. "It's not my place to tell you. But I do need something from you." She looked at Damon.

"What?"

"Do you have any friends in the police force here?"

"Not really. A few in the DA's office. Why?"

"Jennie should be on her way to the hospital right now. I reported her for trying to sell drugs. We need to make sure she stays alive."

Damon processed that and then nodded. "You think that someone put her and Sandra up to this. That it's not just about money."

Tasha didn't respond.

Marco was leaning forward, his dark hair falling over his head. "And if that's true, and they realize we know who Sandra and Jennie are, they may want to get rid of them."

Tasha shrugged. "I think we were intended to find them—this was too easy. The best we can do is to do the unexpected. That means involving the police, which we have been avoiding."

"I'll call the DA's office," Damon said. "Tell them she's a friend's sister. They'll pass that on to the cops. And I'll push my flight back another few days. I need to be back in L.A. by next Sunday. I have court on Tuesday."

Tasha nodded as the limo glided to a stop outside the condo.

"Are you coming up with us?" Marco asked her.

"Yes. It's safer."

Damon wondered who she thought it was safer for—them or herself.

Together they made their way across the elegant lobby. The

security agent looked alarmed until Marco waved and said, "Costume party."

"Of course, Mr. Corzo. There was a food delivery while you were out. Per your standing instructions, we used a master key and placed it in your refrigerator."

"Good man. Food is exactly what we need."

Once in the suite, Damon went to the spare bedroom to gather his things. He'd keep them in Marco's room and sleep on the couch, giving Tasha the bed.

He heard Marco unpacking their forgotten Persian food delivery.

Sitting on the edge of the bed, Damon took a minute to think, looking down at his right hand. He was a big guy, always had been. As a teenager, he'd been so awkward his mother had put away the breakables since he was prone to falling over for no apparent reason. As an adult, he'd learned to control his body, learned to be still and to move slowly—and, when the situation called for it, to use his size to his advantage.

He'd never hit a woman before—outside of sparring in the gym he'd only a hit few people, and only when he was drunk while in college. For the most part, he and his adversaries ended up taking shots together later.

The back of his hand tingled, and he could still feel the blow—the hard bone of her cheek and jaw as he made contact. Part of him was angry at her for asking him to do it, and at himself because he hadn't come up with a better solution.

He stripped off the vest and threw it aside. His self-loathing was made worse by the fact he'd been aroused most of the night. Having Tasha kneeling before him mostly naked, combined with her devotion and obedience, fake though they were, had played on some very base sexual desires. It had been too easy to play her Master, too easy to enjoy spanking her with his belt.

Tasha stood in the doorway, looking at the blond man's bowed shoulders. "Damon."

"Tasha." He stood. Seemingly unsure what to do with his hands, he crossed his arms. "How is your face and your back and your..." He gestured vaguely.

She'd taken off the coat and her shoes, leaving her once more in nothing but the leather bra and tiny shorts. It covered as much as bathing suits, but standing in this bedroom, so close to him, she felt naked—hyperaware of her bare skin. She'd taken off the cuffs but still wore the collar, the leash dangling over her shoulder.

"My ass? All are fine. You were perfect." She came into the room, and without her heels she was almost a head shorter than him. He had a look she'd seen before—guilt over what he'd done in the op. It was the mark of a novice, and it was unexpectedly attractive coming from Damon, who'd been cold and hard before tonight. "Exactly what we needed."

"I wish there'd been a way to do it without me having to hurt you."

"I'm glad it was you and that I didn't have to goad a stranger into doing it."

"Is that what you would have done?"

"Yes."

"But you would have been in real danger—what if the person had choked you or had a knife or—"

"Damon. Stop." Tasha laid a hand on his bare chest. "I was safer tonight with you than I have been in a long time."

His gaze searched her face, then he cupped her head and kissed her.

Tasha froze as his lips covered hers. It was half post-op guilt and half post-op emotional high—it didn't mean anything.

But she didn't care. She wanted him to touch her. Wanted it to mean something.

Tasha clung to his shoulders and let him kiss her. She didn't try to take control, didn't try to goad him into doing something else, something more. For the first time in her life, Tasha let herself be kissed.

Damon pulled back and rested his head on hers.

"I'm sorry. I shouldn't have done that."

Tasha closed her eyes. His words weren't unexpected, but they hurt. Rather than say anything, she turned her back and lifted her hair away from her neck. "You have the key," she said quietly.

"Of course."

He unlocked the collar and slipped it off. Tasha rubbed her neck. "Thank you," she said. "I think Marco has food prepared for you."

Before he could say anything, she left, going to the bathroom. Bracing her hands on the counter, she stared at herself in the mirror. In the bright lights her heavy eye makeup seemed garish. Stripping off the last of her clothes, she looked at her back. There was a faint pink line across her shoulder blades, but her ass was unmarked—it had been well protected by the leather shorts. Part of her wished there was more evidence of what Damon had done. It had taken more concentration than it should have to stay focused on the goal and not let herself give in and enjoy his mastery of her.

She'd never been as attracted to anyone as she was to Damon and Marco. Something about them was different. Or maybe she was just so tired of being alone that she was imagining a connection when there wasn't one. She washed her face, careful of her cheek.

Damon had been right—he was strong, and though she'd pulled away, he'd managed to hit her hard enough that it still hurt—and would bruise. She'd keep it covered so he wouldn't feel any guiltier than he already did.

She jumped into the shower, and when she got out she found her bag outside the bathroom door. By the time she emerged, Damon was asleep on the couch. A plate waited for her on the kitchen counter.

Tasha slid onto a stool and put the plate on her lap. They'd saved her some food, made sure she had her clothes. They'd taken care of her.

Smiling despite herself, Tasha ate quietly while looking at Damon's sleeping form and the lights of the Chicago skyline.

CHAPTER SEVEN

Marco couldn't stay asleep. He'd closed his eyes at three am only to wake up at four thirty. He finally fell asleep again at six but was awake by eight.

Disgusted that he was up before ten for the second day in a row, he tiptoed to the living room where Damon was sleeping.

Except he wasn't. The couch was empty, the blankets neatly folded. Instead, Tasha sat at the dining room table, a variety of electronic equipment spread out in front of her.

At least, Marco assumed the blonde was Tasha.

He ground some beans and turned on the espresso machine, and then leaned his elbows on the counter and examined the woman in his dining room.

She wore basketball shorts, fuzzy socks and a gray T-shirt. Her hair was up in a messy ponytail and there were thick-frame glasses perched on her nose.

"I smell coffee," Damon said as he wandered in.

"Look." Marco motioned to Tasha.

Damon frowned and then filled the espresso machine and

set it brewing. "I thought I dreamed that. At five she came and got me, told me to go sleep in the bed."

"You know I can hear you," Tasha said, not looking up from the screen.

"Do you want coffee?" Damon asked.

"I don't drink coffee."

"Why not?" Marco accepted the espresso cup Damon handed him. He took a sip and a feeling of *rightness* settled over him. This was good—Damon in his kitchen, both of them bantering with Tasha.

"Caffeine is the most addictive drug in the world," she said.

"I don't care," Marco declared.

Tasha smiled and then pulled one leg up and braced her heel on the seat.

"What are you doing?" Damon asked.

"Ignore that," Marco said. "What are you wearing?"

At that she looked over. "I hadn't planned to stay with you, otherwise I would have brought casual clothes more fitting with your perception of me."

"I'm glad you didn't," Marco said. "I like it. Those glasses..." He looked at Damon. "It's not just me, is it?"

Damon was examining her with a look of longing that was painful to see. Marco nudged him and Damon snapped out of it, opening the fridge door. "It's not just you."

"I hate to disappoint you." Tasha pouted and fluttered her lashes. "Actually, I don't care. I need glasses for computer work. And you didn't think I dressed like a call girl all the time, did you?"

"Marco, there is nothing to make breakfast with." Damon closed the fridge. "I'm ordering groceries."

"There's cereal."

Damon just groaned and grabbed the grocery delivery menu.

"You two have been friends a long time, haven't you?" she asked.

"Is it that obvious?" Content to make Damon deal with breakfast, Marco took his espresso over to the table.

"It's nice." She shrugged and went back to her computer.

"So what are you doing?" Marco asked.

Damon finished placing an order and came over to the table, cups in hand. "I made you some herbal tea. If it's disgusting, blame Marco. I have no idea how old the tea is."

Tasha accepted the cup with a little smile. "Thank you. I didn't think either of you would be up so soon. Especially you." She pointed at Marco.

"I can't sleep." Marco finished his coffee. "I need to play."

"It's too early for the piano," Damon said.

"I wasn't going to play piano."

TASHA WATCHED MARCO, who wore PJ pants and nothing more, walk away.

"So what are you doing?" Damon asked again.

Tasha focused on her screen, careful not to look at him. She was still raw from their kiss, and she shouldn't have been. The feelings he'd stirred should've been locked away deep inside, where they couldn't influence her, but right now she couldn't do it.

It had been a deliberate move to wear her lounging clothes. When Tasha was by herself comfort was king, and she didn't care how she looked. She'd brought these things to wear in the hotel, but right now she was using them like armor, distancing herself from the sexy persona she'd been using around them.

"I'm putting up nets for the video and the photos from Marco's phone."

"What does that mean?" he asked.

"How much do you know about how the internet works?"

"I know a bit."

"DNS servers, IP calls?"

"Uh..."

Tasha nodded. "There are lots of things that happen when you do anything online—lots of places the information has to go. There's no way for us to erase the video or photos from existence. Even if I eliminated all online copies, there may be one on a hard drive or other offline location."

Damon sighed. "That's what I've been afraid of."

"We can't delete them, but we can try to stop it from being sent to anyone."

"Using a net?"

"Yes. Every file has some identifying information, some metadata. What I'm doing is setting up alerts so that when a file with that metadata tries to go through any server, it will be flagged. If its point of origin is outside the US the file will have a virus added to it, which will cause most recipients' servers to reject it. If it originates in the US, I can not only attach a virus but also add a back trace."

"That's...wow. You're a very skilled hacker."

"You may not believe it, based on what I've been doing the past few days, but most situations can't be solved with bare skin and sex appeal."

Damon's lips twitched. "Don't tell Marco. He thinks you were a spy. He'll be disappointed when he finds out I was right."

"You were right?"

"You're a corporate securities specialist."

"I hate to disappoint you, but actually Marco was right. I was a spy."

Damon blinked. "You worked for the CIA?"

"Not exactly. I was a CIA asset." Tasha wasn't sure why she was telling him this. Her background was hardly a secret—she'd been something of a legend within the intelligence community—but she rarely divulged personal information. "My biological parents were Russian agents. I was conceived and raised to be a spy for Russia."

Damon sat back. "Holy shit."

Tasha shrugged.

"What happened?"

"My parents were agents who did not love either each other or me. Even as a child I knew it, and therefore I didn't connect with them. I liked reading." Her lips twitched in a smile. "Especially spy novels. When I was twelve I figured out who my parents were. I turned myself in to the CIA."

"When you were *twelve*?"

"Yes."

"What did they do? What did you do?"

"I was a double agent—informing on my parents to my CIA handler. When I started high school I had trouble keeping the secret, and the CIA had them arrested. They were traded back to Moscow."

"All this while you were a teenager?"

"Yes. The CIA pulled me out of school and trained me as an agent, though my background meant I couldn't be formally hired."

Marco, now wearing jeans and a ratty old T-shirt, emerged from the hall, rolling his hard-sided cello case.

Damon was shaking his head. "Let me get this straight. When you were a kid you went to the government and told them you thought your parents were Russian spies. You were right, and they asked you to turn on them, and then when it got too hard they essentially orphaned you by arresting your parents."

"And then they trained me."

Damon's jaw clenched. "That is so deeply fucked up. I'm sorry, Tasha."

She shrugged. "It's done."

The first strains of cello music drew Tasha's attention to the living room. Marco sat with his back to them, facing the wall of windows. His cello cradled in his legs. Tasha bit her lip, thrilled. Abandoning her computer, she padded over and hovered just out of Marco's line of sight so she wouldn't disturb him.

Damon came up behind her. "Have you heard him play before?"

"Once, in London."

"You're a fan."

Tasha felt herself blush and was glad for the thick makeup she was wearing. "I enjoy classical music."

"But Marco doesn't just play music."

"No," she breathed. "He makes it live."

"Come on." Damon grabbed pillows off the couch and drew her to the windows. He tossed the pillows down, sat on the floor facing Marco with his back against the glass and drew Tasha to sit beside him.

She curled up on the pillow. When Damon put his arm around her she leaned into him without thinking about it, her focus wholly on Marco.

He played with his eyes closed and his whole body communicated the emotion he drew from the notes. The low registers were haunting, almost eerie, rising in long, slow swoops to quick, light sounds. Marco tipped his head back as the piece crescendoed, dipped his head and grimaced as his bow powered through the aggressive codas.

When he dropped his arm, the last note lingering in the air, Tasha jumped onto her knees and started clapping.

"Bravo!" she shouted.

Marco looked up. A grin slowly transformed his face. "You enjoyed that?"

"So much." Tasha knew she was being ridiculous, but she couldn't seem to stop herself.

Propping his elbow on his cello, Marco cocked his head. "Any requests?"

"Springtime," she said.

"From my last album?" Marco looked shocked. "That's an original piece of mine and didn't get great reviews."

"I love it. I love that whole album."

"Come here." Marco rose and pushed the chair he'd been sitting on away. Holding the cello with one hand, he dragged the piano bench over and turned it so the short end was against the cello.

He straddled the bench, leaving room between him and the instrument. "Sit here."

Tasha licked her lips. "I shouldn't."

"Why not?"

Giving in, she sat on the end of the bench, her back against Marco's chest, her legs inside the cradle of his.

"Spread your legs," he whispered, scooting them closer to the end.

Arousal washed over her, so sudden and sharp that Tasha was trembling. She cradled the cello between her knees. Marco's arms caged her in and she could feel his breath on her neck.

"Feel the music," he whispered, setting bow to string.

As he began to play, Tasha closed her eyes. Her body swayed with his, and she could feel the faint vibrations of the cello through her knees. He whispered to her as he played, asking her if she could feel the sadness, the joy, the power, putting words to the emotions she'd found in his music.

She was vaguely aware of Damon leaving, but she didn't open her eyes until the last note sounded.

Her breathing was labored as if she'd just gone running, but it wasn't exercise that had caused it—it was desire.

"Tasha." Marco stroked her jaw until she turned her face to his. "I've never seen someone listen to music with their whole mind and heart the way you do."

She was so lost in the moment that she didn't have any words.

Marco kissed her.

For the second time in as many days, she gave in to her desires. Marco's kiss was firmer than Damon's, his lips more demanding. As she shifted, she could feel his cock against her ass. His hand cupped her cheek, holding her still as he went to deepen the kiss.

The pressure against her bruised face shocked her. Tasha pulled back, her gaze meeting Marco's.

"Tasha?"

Shaking her head, she ducked away from him. She wanted to run, but she already looked foolish enough. Forcing herself to walk, she went to the hall. Once there, she bolted for the guest bedroom door and threw it open.

Damon was there, sitting on the edge of the bed, head in hands, as he had been last night.

Tasha took a step back only to smack into Marco. Damon rose to his feet, looking between them.

"I kissed her," Marco said.

"I kissed her last night," Damon added.

The men looked at each other and then at her.

"If you're playing a game," Damon growled, "if you're playing us..."

Tasha opened her mouth to deny it, to tell them that she was terrified because they made her feel things and want things she'd given up on. But they were looking at her with suspicion. How could they do anything else? She was a spy, a liar. They'd seen what she could do, what she would do.

Wishing she were in a little black dress and heels, she folded her arms. "Damon, you need to email the blackmailer back, tell him that you won't pay."

She walked toward the door, praying Marco would move. If he touched her she might start crying.

"And then what?" Damon asked from behind her. There were traces of anger in his voice.

Tasha paused. "There are pieces on the board, and we can see most of them. All we need is for him to make a move."

At the last second, Marco stepped aside. "And you?"

"I will keep working on your problem." Tasha made her way to the living room and packed up her things in record time. Uncaring of who could see, she stripped and put on a designer sheath dress and gold jewelry, transforming herself into a wealthy young society wife.

She knew they'd followed her and could feel their accusing glares on her back as she zipped her bag. Without looking at them, she let herself out of the condo. She didn't start crying until she got to the hotel. Sinking onto the bathroom floor, she pressed a washcloth over her face to muffle the sound of her sobs.

"Looks like you'll have to change your flight again," Marco called out to Damon as he closed the front door.

"Why, who was that?" Damon looked up from his computer. He'd said he was working, but Marco could see that he'd been obsessively refreshing his email to see if the blackmailer had responded.

Marco handed him an envelope. "These just came by messenger."

Damon looked at the creamy envelope and cursed. "We're getting summoned by the Grand Master."

"And it's a formal summons," Marco said. He ripped open the envelope and pulled out the card. It had a date and time embossed in gold. Nothing else. "It's for tomorrow morning."

Damon looked over his shoulder at the late afternoon light. "I'll book us flights and a hotel room for tonight."

Marco nodded and went back to the piano where he started playing a dirge. Damon didn't object, and Marco was sure it was because the funerary music fit the mood in his home. After Tasha had left this morning, he'd been angry—at her, at Damon and at the situation.

But the more time that passed, the more his anger was turning inward. He'd kissed her, not the other way around. Either he'd forced himself on her when her interest was in Damon—which made him insanely jealous of his best friend—or she was interested in both of them, in which case they'd been jerks.

Or the third possibility, the one that haunted him, was that she didn't want anything to do with either of them. That the intimacy Marco felt between them was a product of the situation, and Tasha knew it but was too kind to say anything to them.

Damon turned the card over in his hands. "How badly would it damage your career if you were kicked out of the Trinity Masters?"

Marco sank into a chair and looked at his ring. His life had been defined by his membership. He couldn't imagine being without it. "I don't know. Is that what you think will happen?"

"Formal summons are for invitations to join and being

called to the altar. I doubt the Grand Master has suddenly decided to match us."

"Or that we'd be so lucky as to be in the same trinity." The words were out before Marco could stop them.

Damon looked up sharply, gaze searching Marco's face. Embarrassed, Marco went to make a drink.

"Is that what you want, Marco?"

"It doesn't matter. We're being kicked out."

"But if we weren't, is that what you'd want, for us to be together?"

Marco braced his hands on the bar. "For the sex, I want two women."

Damon snorted. "Of course."

"But the trinity marriage—it's about more than sex. When it comes to sharing my life with someone? I did want it to be you."

Damon rested his hand on Marco's shoulder. Marco braced himself to have his heart broken. He knew Damon didn't see the world the way he did. Or at least he hid his emotions better, ruthlessly crushing anything that couldn't be dealt with easily. What was between them was more than friendship, more than a shared interest in beautiful women.

They were bound together by history, by a unique understanding of one another. It was the most intimate relationship in Marco's life, despite the fact that Damon now lived on the other side of the country.

"I don't want to lose you either," Damon said. They stood that way as the sun dropped behind a building, throwing the room into darkness.

CHAPTER EIGHT

The next morning Marco kept an eye out as Damon keyed in the code to the locked door of the rare book room. #333

Behind the section containing maps and diaries related to the Masonic Temple—an organization with secrets and a history as complex as that of the Trinity Masters—was a section of wall with a triangle inscribed into the plaster. Carved below it were the words *Mitimur in Vetitum.*

We strive for the forbidden.

Damon pushed and the section of wall popped in and slid to the side. Together they stepped into the small room beyond. When the wall clicked back into place the lights turned on.

The wood-paneled walls and carpet of the closet-like space mimicked the other private rooms in the library, meaning anyone who stumbled on it would be shocked but not have a clue as to its true purpose. Marco shifted out of the way as Damon moved the empty book cart that blocked the entrance to the hidden elevator.

"Wait," he said.

The book cart, which was normally empty, had two pieces of paper on it. Marco picked them up, only then seeing that his name was on one, Damon's on the other.

"Box 28," Marco read aloud. He flipped the card over, but there was nothing else.

"Box 29," Damon added.

The wall to their left was inscribed with numbered boxes. They were so skillfully hidden in the wood grain of the paneling that it would be hard for anyone who didn't know they were there to see them. Marco found 28, pressed on it and the box sprang open. Inside was a key and another card.

You'll find garments and a mask in Room A. Right-hand corridor.

Wait until you hear the bell.

—Grand Master

Marco stared at the words in shock.

Damon opened his own box, read the letter and then cursed. "He's got to be fucking kidding me."

Marco licked his lips. "Does this mean…"

"I think so." Damon let out a tired laugh. "We've been called to the altar."

"Together," Marco couldn't help but point out.

Their gazes met and something passed between them—a recognition that their relationship was about to go from devoted friendship to something more.

The elevator was too small to take both of them, so Damon went down first. He was waiting for Marco in the long marble hallway several stories underground.

At the far end were the main gathering rooms. Hallways off each side of the corridor held changing rooms. The ones on the left were for general use when the Trinity Masters had parties or meetings—a place for members to shed themselves of the trappings of the upstairs world—to put on their robes and masks. The hallway on the right housed private dressing rooms for the most elite of members and those who'd been called to the altar.

Marco fit his key into the door of room B. Damon did the same for room A and then looked past Marco at room C. Whomever they'd been mated with was behind that door.

"Why now?" Damon asked. "There has to be a reason."

"Maybe it will solve our problem," Marco said.

"How?"

"I have no idea. This doesn't really make sense."

Damon sighed. "No. It doesn't. But here we are."

Marco saluted his friend and soon-to-be husband and let himself into the dressing room where a hooded black robe waited.

Tasha stared at the white robe draped over the chair in the Grand Master's office.

"What is that?" she yelped.

"Tasha, it is time for you to join in a trinity."

Her stomach rolled and Tasha took a step back. "No. You can't be serious."

"I am."

She met the Grand Master's gaze, anger making her words tremble. "Don't pretend that I'm like the rest of them. I have nothing to offer a trinity. All I am is your little soldier."

"Natasha," he barked her name. "This is not a matter for debate. You knew the rules when you joined."

"And you knew I was dying inside, and still you asked me to do your dirty work." Anger she thought she'd buried years ago bubbled up. "You can't change that now."

The Grand Master's hand closed into a fist. "I'm giving you

the courtesy of telling you in person that you've been called to the altar, rather than simply issuing a summons. I will give you a moment to get dressed. You're welcome to use my office. Then you will go to the altar room for the presentation ceremony where you will meet your spouses."

Tasha felt like she was choking. The need to lash out crawled along her skin and her fingers curled into claws. Before she could do something she couldn't take back, Tasha grabbed the robe from the chair and stormed out of the office.

"Natasha," the Grand Master warned.

She marched along the hall that connected his office with the rest of the headquarters. She stopped before a door she'd never gone through before—the Grand Master's entrance to the ritual room.

Natasha threw open the door. Beyond it was a stone room, much smaller and more intimate than the massive gathering room. The floor and walls were marble and three high-backed wing chairs faced a large metal medallion in the center of the floor. Each chair was illuminated by a rectangle of light. Two chairs were occupied by figures in black robes—two men.

The Grand Master thought that after everything she'd done for him he could suddenly match her? Worse, he wanted her to marry two men, rather than the man and woman she'd dreamed of? She didn't know anything about being a wife. She needed another woman to show her what to do.

"Leave," Tasha told them. "You don't want this." She threw the white robe onto the medallion in the floor. "Whoever you are, you're about to be trapped, married to the Grand Master's pet spy." Tasha hadn't been this angry in a long time. She tried to rein it in, but everything that had taken place in Chicago was right there on the surface, muting her ability to retreat to the emotionless place where she functioned best.

"Natasha Kasharin," the Grand Master's voice echoed from behind her. "You are out of line."

"I will not spend my life married to people who hoped for power, intelligence and wealth from their partners only to find themselves married to a whore, a liar and a killer." Tears choked her, and she dug her nails into her palms to fight them back. "I took your pity once, I won't do it again."

Tasha faced the men again. "Leave," she said, meaning it to be strong, but it came out as a plea.

One at a time, they rose. Tasha breathed a sigh of relief—they'd listened, they'd go.

"Tasha."

Her heart stopped when she heard the voice. She shook her head. "No." It couldn't be.

Marco threw back his hood. "Tasha, it's us."

Damon did the same.

She whirled to the Grand Master, her mind racing. "You're...you're punishing them for falling into his trap." She looked back at Marco and Damon. "You're punishing them...with me."

"Natasha, that is not it. I chose to join you with them because it's clear that you have a connection. A connection you've never had with any other member that you've helped. When I found out that you included them in your plans, I knew you trusted them. This is not punishment—for any of you."

Tasha laughed bitterly. "It's not? Marco, who should have an elegant, sophisticated wife, would instead be stuck with me, who can only pretend to be something good and pure. And Damon—he will never become a federal judge if he is associated with me. I'm the daughter of spies. No one will care that I gave up everything for this country."

"Tasha," Damon said. "I'm so glad it's you."

She gasped, his words like a knife to her heart. He couldn't mean that.

"Tasha, come here," Marco coaxed. "Take a deep breath, beautiful."

"No." The word trembled on her lips. "No. I won't let you do this to them."

She ran, brushing by the Grand Master. She knew all the exits from this place and took the one into a water main that dumped into the harbor. It was for the most dire emergencies—which this was. Three blocks later, wet to her waist, Tasha climbed out through a manhole. She ducked into the first clothing store she could find, bought new clothes and then changed. She walked quickly and jumped on a bus, resorting to tradecraft—spy behavior—without even having to think about it.

Two hours later, she was on a Greyhound headed to Oklahoma. It was time to go home.

DAMON STARED in shock at the darkness into which Tasha had disappeared. So many things had just happened that he had trouble deciding which he should focus on—the fact that Tasha was going to be their wife, her assertion that the Grand Master had arranged the match as some sort of punishment, or her belief that she wasn't good enough for them.

The last one caused the guilt he felt over the way they'd confronted her to thicken in his gut. He'd seen little hints of the vulnerable woman who'd just stormed from the room. And yet he'd still acted as if she were plotting something by having kissed them both.

"Don't just stand here," the Grand Master said. "Go after her."

"Wait." It was Marco who spoke. "You need to tell us what's really going on."

There was a beat of silence. "I don't *need* to do anything."

"That's our future wife," Damon added. "What did she mean when she said she took your pity?"

The Grand Master, who stood in darkness, sighed. It was the most human thing Damon had ever heard him do. "Her CIA handler was a member. When it became clear that Tasha could not survive as an asset for much longer, her handler, who was himself retiring, asked that she be made a member. Tasha is...unlike anyone else. She never had a normal life, and yet she knows more about people than anyone I've ever met. I should have paired her right away. I knew she was excited about a marriage, excited because she would get to be part of something that to her would seem normal."

"A trinity marriage?" Damon asked. "That was normal?"

"Marriage, planning a future, being intimate—they were things she said she didn't know how to do. She even asked me if she could be paired with a man and a woman, so that she would have someone to teach her how to be a wife."

"Jesus," Marco breathed.

"Then why us, and why now?" Damon said. "Why not then, when she wanted it?"

There was silence before the Grand Master said, "There are things happening that you don't know about. We're under attack and have been for years. Tasha had no ties, nothing to lose. She was...not wrong in accusing me of using her the way the CIA did."

"And why didn't you match her?"

"Because I know the members of this society, and I knew that once she was married, her spouses would move heaven and earth to protect her—even from me."

"And you're damned, fucking right," Damon growled.

"Stay away from her," Marco added.

"Don't forget who you're talking to." The Grand Master's words dripped with warning.

"We won't forget," Marco said. "We just don't care."

They turned for the doors to the dressing rooms.

"I have an address. A place she thinks I don't know about," the Grand Master said.

Damon paused but didn't turn at his words.

"I will send it to you."

"Fine." Marco ripped open the door.

"I expect you back here in one month," the Grand Master said. "To be formally married."

"Let's hope we catch her by then." Damon disappeared into the dressing room.

As he threw off the robe and put on his clothes, he was grinning. Despite the seriousness of the situation he was excited. When he joined Marco in the hall he saw the same expression on his best friend's face.

"Want to go catch and marry a reformed Russian spy?" Marco asked.

Damon laughed. "As long as we can do it before Sunday. I've got to go to work."

"A lawyer and a musician? I'm sure we'll have no trouble finding a highly trained intelligence agent."

MARCO LOOKED at the pretty yellow farm house and then back to Damon. "Do you think the Grand Master is testing us?"

"This is certainly not what I expected."

They were in the middle of Oklahoma, deep in farm country. The road they were on didn't have a name and the house didn't have a number. They'd stopped in the little town off the freeway and asked for the scientist's house, which is what the Grand Master's instructions had said. They'd been given directions that included abandoned tractors and big trees instead of street names. Strangely, it hadn't been that hard to find. There was no other house in sight. The only other structures were some massive poly-tunnel green houses. It was just before noon and they'd been traveling since five am—they hadn't been able to get flights yesterday but had been on the first flights out this morning. The day was taking on a surreal feel. Marco wouldn't have been surprised if a little old lady had walked out onto the porch holding a cherry pie.

"Well, we might as well knock." Damon started up the steps.

Marco put his hand out. "Wait." He stepped to the side, searching for the hint of movement he'd seen. "I think there's someone in that poly tunnel."

"The what?" Damon asked as they rounded the house, taking a path back to the plastic and metal structures.

"That's a poly tunnel."

"Why do you know that?"

"When I'm bored I watch educational programming."

Damon snorted. "I can't believe I'm stuck with you for the rest of my life."

Marco grinned. "I keep forgetting."

"It feels weird to say it," Damon admitted.

"Weird bad or weird good?"

"Weird good."

The door to the closest greenhouse was open. Moving quietly, they crept to where they could get a better look.

A slim blonde woman wearing brown overalls and a white tank top was bent over a raised bed of plants. She was holding a little metal box with a probe on it, which she stuck into the soil. After a second, she picked up a clipboard and made a note. Her hair was pulled back in a simple braid and covered with a navy-blue bandana.

As she turned, Marco caught a glimpse of her profile—Tasha.

"That's Tasha," Damon said. "Damn. I didn't think I could be surprised again."

Marco agreed. People were complex, but Tasha was a whole new level of complicated—from the sexy spy to the eccentric hacker and now the wholesome farm girl.

Without looking up, she said, "You might as well come in. I know you're there."

Marco led the way, entering the poly tunnel, which was humid and smelled of growing things. Inside it seemed even bigger—there were rows and rows of tables, each covered in lush green plants.

"Hello, Tasha," he said.

She set down her clipboard and started picking dead leaves off the closest greenery.

"How did you know we were here?" Damon asked, folding his arms. He was wearing a suit and was already looking damp. Marco had on slacks and a dress shirt. They were both overdressed, but at least he wasn't wearing a jacket.

"I'm not so stupid as to think that I can't be found. Even here."

"And where is here?" Marco asked. Tasha still hadn't looked at them.

"My home," she said simply.

"This is where you live—in the middle of Oklahoma?"

"I have condos in other cities. I don't get to spend all my time here."

"But why here?" Damon asked.

Tasha wandered away from them down one of the aisles,

fingers gently brushing the leaves. "I have a degree in agricultural engineering."

Marco rocked back on his heels. He hadn't expected that.

"It's funny," she continued, "because that's what my parents wanted me to major in. That was part of their plan for me—probably some sort of bio-terrorism plot. When I got out of the CIA, I finished school—high school—and then went to college sporadically. I didn't plan to study ag, especially since that's what my parents had wanted, but all my best memories growing up were centered around plants and farming. I know now that they were building my interest in the subject deliberately, but when I was little all I knew was that we had fun when we went to farms or planted things in the garden."

Marco's heart ached for Tasha. He wasn't particularly close with his family, but he knew they loved him and were proud of him. Damon was very close to his parents, but they'd retired from their medical practice a few years ago and joined the Peace Corps. They were now running a clinic in Africa. They may not be close to their families, but they knew they were loved and supported by them.

"Tasha," he asked. "Why did you run?"

She didn't answer. Marco looked at Damon, who jerked his head. Marco nodded in understanding and then went after Tasha.

"Tasha." He closed the gap between them.

"I shouldn't have run," she said. "I was upset when I needed to be calm. What I was trying to explain is that the Grand Master feels guilty for asking me to use my training. But now, after all the things I've done, I'm not a good match for anyone." She crossed her arms over her belly, hugging herself. "When I realized it was the two of you, I knew the Grand Master was trying to solve two problems at the same time—he could punish you and assuage his guilt over me by binding us together."

"Tasha, look at me." Marco gently grabbed her arm.

She tried to pull away, but Damon had circled around and was blocking her retreat.

"You're not our punishment," Marco whispered. "And you're the most amazing, beautiful, interesting woman I've ever met."

"Don't say that," she whispered, dipping her head. "Don't."

"It's true." Damon tucked his finger under her chin and lifted her face. In an instant, his expression changed from cajoling to horrified. "What did I do to you?" he asked.

Marco leaned so he could see her right cheek—which he realized she'd kept turned away from them. It was black and blue from her temple to her jaw.

Damon had his hands on his head, pressing the heels of his hands against his temples. "Fuck. No wonder she ran away. Look what I fucking did."

"Damon, no, that's not it." Tasha reached for him, but pulled her hand back. "It's fine, I just didn't get a chance to put makeup on."

"Makeup? Did it look like this that morning? Were you sitting in the condo with your face all beat up?" he asked.

Her silence was damning.

Damon stormed out of the greenhouse. Tasha's shoulders sagged. Marco felt sick seeing her face like that—bruised and battered. Tasha was undoubtedly the most capable person he'd ever met, and he was sure that if they were to find themselves in a dangerous situation she'd be the one to get them out. Yet, against all reason, he wanted—no, needed—to protect her. And he needed to protect Damon.

"Come on," Marco said.

"Just go." Tasha pulled away, but there was no anger, no fight, in her words, just sadness.

"No. I'm not going anywhere without you, both of you." Marco took her hand and dragged her after him. His spouses were hurting, and he was going to fix them.

Marco had no idea how to do that. He was an experienced lover but a novice husband and boyfriend. He'd never really thought about how he'd manage the relationship side once he was finally married. Maybe he should have.

Then again, even in his wildest dreams he hadn't imagined he'd be paired with his best friend and a dangerous and damaged former spy.

Damon was sitting on the porch steps, staring at their rental car. When Marco dragged Tasha up he stood, gaze focused on Tasha's face. In the daylight it looked worse—her skin was maroon and purple, her eye a bit swollen.

"I knew I'd fucked it up," he said. "I knew I hit you too hard."

"You didn't." Tasha shook off Marco's hold. "Truly, this is exactly what I thought would happen. You were right. If you'd really connected you could have easily broken my jaw."

"I hit you." Damon thumped down onto the step, head in his hands. "I hit my wife. I'm like some sort of fucked-up white-trash cliché."

"Your...wife."

Marco watched Tasha as she whispered the word wife. She looked both terrified and happy. He held on to that hint of happiness. She wanted to be with them. He could see it on her face.

Putting his arm around her, Marco kissed her head. "That's right, you're our wife."

She swallowed. "Both of you."

"Yes."

Licking her lips, she looked away. "No. I'm sorry, but we can't do this. I would ruin your futures. You deserve—"

"What we *want*," Marco cut in. "Is you. We both do. That's why we kissed you."

"But then you were mad."

"That's because we're morons." Marco said it so matter-of-factly that Tasha let out a startled little laugh. "Well, I'm a moron. He's an abuser."

"Fuck you, dude," Damon moaned without looking up. "Seriously, fuck you."

Tasha broke out into deep belly laughs. She staggered to the steps, took a seat by Damon and leaned against his leg. He looked up, reached out a tentative hand and rested it on her shoulder.

She looked back at him. "It doesn't hurt, and it's actually better than I expected."

"You asked me to hit you thinking that your face would be even more bruised than this?"

"Yes. Look at the size of you."

"Then why did you ask? I knew I shouldn't have done it."

"I meant what I said that night. If it wasn't you it would have been someone else, and then it might not have ended so well."

"We'll never let anyone hurt you again," Marco said, drawing her attention.

She opened her mouth as if to argue but then just shook her head.

The tension had abated somewhat when she sat on the steps, but now it ratcheted back up. Marco looked between Tasha and Damon.

"Hit him," he said.

They both focused on him. "What?" Damon asked.

"Tasha, hit him back. He'll feel better."

She rolled her eyes. "I'm not going to hit him back."

"Yeah, because she's a good person, not an asshole," Damon muttered.

Tasha's brow rose. "Actually, my objection is that it would hardly be fair. I don't have your upper-body strength. I wouldn't be able to hit as hard as you did."

Damon groaned. "I'm so sorry."

"I'll hit him for you," Marco offered.

"You might hurt your hands," Tasha scolded. "Don't be silly."

Marco considered that. "What if you used a weapon?"

"Uh..." Damon was starting to look alarmed.

"What kind of weapon?" Tasha asked, her tone calm and curious.

"Whatever seems fair. I assume you know more about weapons than me." Marco had a bad feeling he was losing control of this situation.

"I have quite a few—knives, clubs, some more exotic ones, though those are for show."

"A knife seems a bit extreme."

She tipped her head in a considering manner. "I have a bean-bag gun."

Marco nodded. "That seems fair, doesn't it?"

Damon threw his hands in the air. "Not the face—I have to go to court."

Tasha patted his shoulder as she went into the house. Marco tried and failed to hide his grin.

"You're an ass," Damon said.

"No, I'm not. I know you—you'll obsess about this unless you feel that you've paid for your crime."

"Okay, maybe. But you don't have to look so happy about it."

"Someday you will see how funny this is."

"It's not funny. Look what I did to her face."

"And if it was anyone but you who'd done it I'd kill them. But you didn't hit her out of anger or rage. It was part of a plan. Her plan. You're the one who said we had to trust her expertise."

"I know I did, but when I said that I didn't...I didn't care about her."

"The way you do now?"

Damon nodded. "And you?"

"The same."

The screen door squeaked as it opened. Tasha had what looked like a thick-barreled shot gun resting on her shoulder.

"You look like a sexy redneck," Marco said.

"Thank you...I think." Tasha came down the steps and turned to face Damon. "Where do you want it?"

He rose and stripped off his jacket. "Chest, I guess."

She brought the rifle to her shoulder. "Ready?"

Marco balled his hands into fists. It had seemed funny a minute ago, but that gun was larger and more threatening than he'd expected. Marco had feelings for Tasha—he desired and wanted to protect her. But he loved Damon.

"Yes." Damon's arms were at his sides, jaw set.

Tasha glanced over at Marco. "And you?"

Marco looked at Damon, who nodded. He forced himself to relax. "Yes."

Tasha dropped the gun. "You were really going to let me shoot him?" she asked Marco.

"You're not going to?"

"No. Of course not. I expected you to stop me. It's clear you love each other."

Marco was shocked by her words—shocked that she'd labeled what was between them that way. He did love Damon, but he didn't think anyone else could see that.

"We're just…" Damon's words trailed off. "I mean that we didn't…we've never…"

Marco wanted to shake him. "You're right," he said to Tasha. "We do love each other. Because we're friends. We get each other. But we didn't expect we'd be in the same trinity."

"And now you are," Tasha said.

"Yes." Damon came up to where they stood. "And so are you. We're in it together."

Tasha shook her head. "I'm sorry, but I won't do it. I won't marry you. Either of you."

CHAPTER NINE

Tasha couldn't help but be relieved when they followed her into the house. She wasn't giving them a reason to stay, yet they were. It was hard not to read into that, not to get her hopes up.

Tasha still couldn't believe that Damon would have let her shoot him—bean-bag rounds hurt. More than that, she couldn't believe Marco would have let her do it. She'd seen the way the other man tensed and moved towards Damon, as if to protect him.

They were a unit, a pair. The fact that their friendship had just been turned into a marriage only strengthened that bond. Tasha could imagine that a different woman would hate the situation—would fear being left out of that relationship. But not Tasha.

On the bus ride here she'd realized that their relationship did what she'd wanted when she'd requested she be matched with a man and a woman. All her life she'd learned to quickly form and then dissolve relationships of all kinds. She had no idea what a real one looked or felt like—her parents certainly weren't good role models—and she'd been terrified of having to try to create that. With these two she didn't have to. They already loved each other.

Maybe it didn't matter that they'd never love her.

Shaking her head, she opened the gun cabinet—the visible one where she kept legally purchased firearms—and put the bean-bag gun in there.

"Tasha," Marco said. "Just because we know each other, and yes, we love each other, doesn't have any effect on our trinity. Damon and I have to have a new kind of relationship, one that includes you—just because we know each other doesn't mean we're not going to love you."

"That's not what I'm worried about," she said, ignoring the way the word love made her heart race.

"Then why did you say no?"

"What I said in the ceremony room was true. Marrying me would be a punishment. It would mean your careers wouldn't advance the way you were promised when you joined."

"We're not talking about that." Damon loosened his tie and rolled up his sleeves, looking very much like the hard-working lawyer, while Marco was all casual dark elegance.

"I am," she said.

"Tasha." Damon stuffed his hands in his pockets. "If you don't want to be with us because of what we've done in our pasts then please just tell us. If that's the case we won't fight with you about this."

"What do you mean?" she asked, confused.

"You know we're not exactly choir boys. We haven't always been the most respectful towards women—the orgies maybe weren't our finest hour."

"Speak for yourself," Marco muttered.

"You think..." Tasha raised her eyebrows. It was too absurd.

She went into the kitchen, took three mismatched glasses from a cupboard and poured them all water. "You think I'm fabricating reasons for saying I won't marry you as a way to cover the fact that I don't *want* to be with the two of you?"

"Yeah, I do," Damon said.

Looking between the two undeniably handsome, sexy men, Tasha could only shake her head. "Any woman in the Trinity Masters would be lucky to have you. Which is why you shouldn't be matched with me."

She went through the living room to the first-floor bedroom and closed the door. She took off her overalls and pulled on a pair of leggings, a long nubby sweater coat and fuzzy socks. Back in the living room, she wasn't surprised to see that they were still there, but their reaction to her return caught her off-guard. Each man rose to his feet, looking her up and down.

"You're the most beautiful woman I've ever seen," Marco said.

"Absolutely," Damon agreed.

Tasha looked down at herself. She hadn't consciously meant to be alluring, but if she were honest with herself she would admit that she'd gone for an approachable-girlfriend-hanging-out-on-the-weekend look.

Marco sat on the couch and patted the cushion next to him. Ignoring that, she took a seat in an armchair that matched the one Damon sat in.

There was quiet stillness between them for the first time since they met.

"Do you know what the greatest threat to women is?" Tasha asked, surprised at herself.

They both shook their heads.

"Men." Tasha wrapped her sweater coat around herself. "Historically and even currently, a woman is at her most vulnerable when she's with a man—her father, brother, husband."

They shared a confused glance but didn't interrupt.

"Ever since I was young I've learned how to manipulate people. Not control them the way someone like the Grand Master controls us, but manipulate them nonetheless. Because I'm pretty and young and blonde, usually I was asked to manipulate men."

"Tasha, you don't have to tell us about your past," Marco said.

"But if you want to you can," Damon added. "Nothing you can say will change anything, will change how we feel about you."

"My past is my own," she said quietly. "This isn't about that. What I'm trying to say is I know, maybe more than anyone, how vulnerable a woman is around men. My skills and training protect me. That night at the club I was manipulating the situation." She motioned to her cheek. "I manipulated Damon into hitting me when that goes against his nature. I manipulated the rest of the people in the club into focusing on me. But I was not really in control. I was vulnerable."

Unable to sit still, she started to pace. Piece by piece, she peeled back layers of justification and defenses, telling them things about her fears that she only barely admitted to herself.

"The only way I know how to protect myself is with manipulation. I can become anyone or anything that I need to in order to get what I want."

"That was your job," Damon said.

"It was, but it's also who I am." Tasha twisted her fingers together to hold her hands still. "I don't think I'm a good match for anyone—especially the elite members of the Trinity Masters. I've known that I wasn't going to be part of a trinity for years. That made me sad, but I knew it had to be that way. Not only because my past and my reputation would ruin anyone associated with me, but..."

She sighed, shoulders sagging. "But because I knew if I was paired with a man, I couldn't stop myself from manipulating him in order to protect myself. I would change who I was every day, every hour, in order to be who or what I thought he wanted." She forced herself to resume her seat. "When I joined, I thought maybe having another woman in the trinity would help that. Would give me someone to copy, a model to base myself on. It wouldn't really be me—I'd be playing a role, but I might be safer."

"You will always be safe with us," Damon said quietly.

"Even from myself?"

Marco rose, sleek and dark like a panther in human form, and held out one hand. "Tasha, come here."

She looked at his outstretched hand, fighting tears. She wanted to take his hand, wanted to believe she could be the kind of woman who could take what he was offering.

"Tasha." His tone was soft, but there was a hint of command.

You can pretend, just for a little while.

Unfolding her legs, Tasha rose tentatively. There was a hush in the room, as if the whole world was watching her, waiting to see if she'd take what was offered. But it wasn't the whole world watching her and Marco, it was just Damon, his hazel eyes intent on her.

Tasha slipped her hand into Marco's.

He drew her against his chest, sliding his hands under her sweater to rest on her lower back. She was instantly aroused, aware.

"Do you trust me?" Marco asked.

"No," she said, completely honest.

"That's fair. Will you let me kiss you?"

"You didn't ask before."

"This time I am."

"And if I say no?"

"Then I will respect that, but I will be very sad. Kissing you is all I've been able to think about since you stormed into the ceremony room. Have you thought about kissing me?"

"No," she lied.

"Have you thought about kissing Damon?"

"No." This time her voice quavered a little. She was an excellent liar. What was wrong with her?

Marco roamed his hand up her back and then down to her ass. "Have you thought about Damon and I kissing you at the same time?"

Tasha's whole body was thrumming with arousal. It was making her lightheaded. She'd never felt like this before. She leaned away from Marco.

Her back hit something warm and solid.

Damon was there, his size all too apparent as he stood behind her, crowding her toward Marco.

"Have you thought about Damon and I doing other things to you, with you?"

Damon spread his hands over her belly, his thumbs just below the lower swell of her breasts. A vivid image of them in this same position, except naked, popped into her head. It terrified and aroused her. For all her experience, being with them would be something new, something foreign.

But there was something she had to tell them.

Sighing, Tasha grabbed one forearm each and twisted, breaking free of their hold before they had a chance to react. Both men stumbled back, surprise clear on their face.

"Too fast," Damon said.

Marco nodded. "My fault. I'm sorry, Tasha."

"It's not that. There's something else you should know…

about me." She pointed to the couch and they sat shoulder to shoulder.

She perched on the edge of a chair, resting her elbows on her knees. Looking at her men—*my men? Did I really just think that?*—she realized when they'd followed her into the house she'd started to accept their trinity was real. She'd run, giving them the perfect out, giving the Grand Master every reason to reconsider. But they'd come for her. They hadn't let her push them away.

Tasha was tired of running, of hiding. She knew it wouldn't last, knew that someday she'd be proved right and they'd want the world-class careers and lives that came with being a member of the Trinity Masters. But right now they wanted her—she believed that much. And she wanted them too.

"There's something you need to know about me."

"Like we said, your past is your own. You don't have to tell us anything, but if you do, it won't change how we feel about you."

Tasha smiled at Damon's serious words. She wanted to see him in a courtroom. She bet he'd be great.

"Thank you. I won't tell you everything. Actually, I won't tell you much, but if we're going to do this—"

"We are," Marco said.

"Then you should know that technically I'm a virgin."

DAMON LEANED FORWARD and peered at Tasha. "I'm sorry, I think I misheard you. For a minute I thought you said you were a virgin."

Tasha blinked those big blue eyes at him. "I am. Technically."

Marco moaned quietly. Damon swallowed hard and sat back.

That was the fucking sexiest thing he'd ever heard. His dick was iron hard inside his pants. Right now Tasha looked innocent enough to be a virgin—she had no makeup on, her hair was back in a braid and she wore a tank top and leggings that showed off her body without being sexy.

But this was the same woman who'd taken them to a BDSM club, who'd played his submissive so astutely he'd felt like he owned her.

Silence stretched out, and Tasha started to look worried.

"Are you two okay?"

"Processing," Damon said. "Trying not to jump across the room and grab you."

"You...like the fact that I'm a virgin?" She tipped her head to the side. "Of course. Once I turned twenty-two I stopped doing the virgin schoolgirl, so I forgot what kind of reaction that could get."

"How are you a virgin?" Marco asked. "And what do you mean technically?"

"I was trained in tradecraft—that's basically spy school. I learned all kinds of technical and computer-based hacking and development, how to hide who I am and what I was doing and sexual behaviors and manipulation."

Damon was trying and failing not to imagine her in some sexy schoolgirl uniform.

"I was fifteen when I started."

"You were a minor?" Damon's arousal died a hard death. "That's despicable."

She shrugged. "I stopped being a child when I turned in my parents."

"That doesn't mean they had the right to manipulate your sexuality at such a young age."

"There was a need for someone who could attract targets whose sexual interests ran to children. They taught me how to be innocent in a way that older men found attractive and also how to keep myself from actually being touched."

She sighed. "Almost all my training was about how to look or act like a fantasy without ever letting anyone get close to me. I attended PhD-level classes with a human sexuality expert and apprenticed with a dominatrix. It was a very thorough education not only about the physical actions of sex, but the mental and emotional impulses. When I was seventeen, I went to Istanbul to a famous brothel. They taught me how to play a sexual submissive and about the different kinds of kinks and subcultures. I was good at what I did—I've played the little girl in pigtails for many men. I was even sold at auction in Beirut."

"Sold...as a sex slave?" Marco's hands clenched. "You could have been killed."

"True." She looked between them and the horror Damon felt must have shown on his face. "If it makes you feel better, for six months I was the mistress of a whorehouse."

"I'm not sure if that's hot or horrifying," Damon said.

"My feelings exactly," Marco added. "Tasha, if you did all this, why do you think you're a virgin?"

"I told you—I was the fantasy. My skill was in keeping the target engaged and wanting. If I had sex with them then there was no allure. If I gave them what they wanted then they might lose interest."

"But if you were a sex slave or a submissive, how did you manage?"

Tasha smiled. "I know how to top from the bottom—how to make the owner or daddy or Dom feel like they're in control when really I'm manipulating them. I'm not saying that I'm inexperienced sexually or that I've never gotten a spanking, whipping or had a variety of toys used on me, but I always managed to hold back that last piece. Always managed to keep them wanting more."

At the mention of a whipping, Damon's stomach rolled. He was trying to ignore her bruised face, trying not to focus on how much he hated himself for doing that to her. But hearing this, all he could think about was that he was no better than the men she'd known before.

"So you've never..." Marco seemed to be struggling with what she was saying.

"I've never had intercourse with another person." She shrugged. "That probably doesn't matter, I mean what's the difference between a man's fingers or a dildo and a real cock?"

"Uh, there's a big difference," Damon said.

She smiled. "That's always what I told myself. It's stupid to think that just because I've never let a man fuck me that I'm virginal." She laughed softly. "Virgin implies innocent. I'm not."

"I want to say something profound and meaningful," Marco whispered to Damon, "but I can't get the image of her using a dildo on herself out of my head."

Damon understood his friend's problem. He was an uncomfortable mix of horrified and aroused. He wanted to drag Tasha to the floor and fuck her until her toes curled, but at the same time he wanted to wrap her up and promise her that no one would ever touch her again.

"Marco? Damon? Are you okay?"

Damon realized they'd been sitting there staring at her for five minutes. "We, uh, are taking some time to process what you said."

She nodded and looked away. He could see the hurt in her eyes.

"Tasha." Damon got up and sat on the coffee table, close enough to touch her. "You're not like anyone I've ever met before. I don't want to hurt you again, and right now I'm terrified to even touch you." Damon let his hand hover over hers but didn't make contact. "I don't want to be like anyone you've been with before. I'm your husband. You're my wife. Do you know what that means?"

"I have no idea. I never have."

"It means that I, actually that we—Marco and I—will protect you, love you and care for you. That includes satisfying you sexually, whatever that means. All we need to know is what you're comfortable with. Not what you were trained to do. Not what you think we want. What do you, Tasha, desire?"

She looked startled. Then she started to blink rapidly. Before he knew it, a tear rolled down her cheek. His previous hesitation forgotten, Damon scooped her up and carried her to the couch to set her down on his lap. Marco scooted over, taking her legs onto his knee and stroking her calves.

"Why are you crying, beautiful?" Marco asked softly.

"I'm scared."

"Of us?"

"Yes. Of all of it."

She was shivering, and Damon hugged her closer. "We won't hurt you."

"Don't put me in the middle," she pleaded. "It's too much pressure. I won't be able to do it without pretending to be someone, something, else."

Damon looked at Marco. Don't put me in the middle.

Did that mean what he thought it did?

MARCO STROKED Tasha's legs as he processed her whispered plea. After everything she'd said—her extensive sexual training, her fear that she'd become manipulative because that's how she protected herself—it made sense that she was scared of being put in the middle. It was a lot of pressure. Marco hadn't even realized that he'd assumed Tasha's place in their sexual relationship would be between them.

He met Damon's gaze, and for the first time he looked at his friend as more than a companion. He looked at him as a lover.

"If you don't want to be in the middle," Marco said to Tasha, keeping his gaze on Damon, "then we won't put you there."

She looked up, her head resting on Damon's shoulder. Marco liked seeing them together. They would have beautiful blonde children.

He'd have to come back to that idea later.

"You mean..." Damon's face was set, his eyes stormy.

"Yes."

Tasha looked between them. "You've been lovers?"

"No."

"No."

"Do you want to be lovers?" she asked.

Marco didn't answer. He feared admitting that he did want to be Damon's lover would scare his friend.

"We're friends," Damon said, sounding frustrated. "We've never...I mean, we've had sex with the same woman, at the same time."

"That's what you thought you'd use me for. A way to be together without touching." She sounded tired.

"No," Marco assured her. "We both knew there was a possibility that we would be part of a trinity with another man. Bisexuality is practically a requirement of the Trinity Masters." His gaze met Damon's. "But this is complicated. Like you said, we do love each other—as friends and companions. I'm always happiest when Damon's with me. Adding sex to that is daunting."

Damon looked embarrassed, but he nodded in agreement.

Tasha's face lit up. "So you're like a romantic comedy. The kind where two friends realize they're meant for each other." She looked excited.

"We are not a romantic comedy." Damon's teeth were gritted.

"It sounds like a romantic comedy."

"I'm starting to worry that you have terrible taste in movies," Marco added.

"I love romantic comedies. And Nicholas Sparks books."

"That's it. Forget it. I'm not marrying her," Marco declared, lips twitching.

Tasha smiled. "I think you're stuck with me."

"Does that mean you're agreeing to the marriage?" Always the lawyer, Damon was trying to close the deal.

"Yes...maybe. If you two promise that you won't put me in the middle. I don't think I can handle it. Not right away. If we're going to do this, then I want to be me...just me. I'm not even sure I know how to do that, but I'd like to try."

"And that's what we want too." Marco stroked the outside of her thigh and then laced his fingers with Damon's so she was cradled between them.

"Damon?"

His friend nodded and then rose while still holding Tasha. "Where's the bedroom?"

DAMON FOLLOWED TASHA'S DIRECTIONS, carrying her up the stairs, which creaked under him. Marco opened the door.

The bedroom was like something out of a country calendar. The bed was a large four-poster with a white crochet cover. There was a large dark-wood armoire against one wall and simple armchair in the counter. He set Tasha on her feet. She pulled the sweater around herself.

"This is the master bedroom," she said. "I never use it. I don't have guests. But there are sheets. I like making up the room. It makes me feel homey."

"It's a nice place." Damon felt like an idiot. He had no idea what to do, what to say.

Tasha looked at him. "You don't have to do this if you don't want to."

Marco slid his hand across his back and Damon froze. Desire flooded him, unexpected and exciting. He closed his eyes.

"He needs time to process this," Marco said. "He's a bit of a straight arrow."

Damon didn't respond. The reality was that as far as sex with a man went, he was a virgin—and as far as he knew Marco was too.

Marco stepped up behind him, his chest against Damon's back. Tasha's gaze was fixed on them, and she was biting her lower lip.

One by one, Marco undid the buttons of Damon's shirt. Damon held still, struggling to understand his feelings. He was aroused and nervous. He had this terrible feeling that if he didn't keep himself still he would turn and devour Marco. He'd always been a careful lover—his size made that a necessity. It was easy to be gentle with women. Their femininity automatically triggered that. But he was about to have sex with Marco—his friend, his companion in debauchery. There was no need for gentleness.

"Damon," Marco whispered in his ear. "It's just me."

"I don't want to hurt you," he growled.

"Hurt me?"

"Yes, damn it."

He saw Tasha leave the room, but right now he couldn't focus on her. He was focused on Marco.

Turning, he fisted his hand in Marco's hair. His blue eyes were heavy with arousal. "I never thought we'd do this," Damon admitted.

"I hoped. I've wanted you for a long time."

"Why didn't you say anything?"

"What was the point? We were going to be married to other people. Starting a relationship would have just made that harder."

"I don't find men attractive," Damon said. "Except you."

"I'm glad you think I'm pretty." Marco grinned that teasing half smile that normally made Damon roll his eyes.

Damon kissed him. He kissed that smile he'd seen so many times. Marco was stiff, surprised, but then he grabbed the back of Damon's shirt. They fought for control of the kiss. As Damon feared, they were not gentle with each other. Sex demanded that someone submit, but neither was willing to do that—not yet.

Damon ripped Marco's shirt open, sending buttons flying. Marco undid his belt, tossed it aside and fumbled with his pants. Urging Marco back toward the bed, Damon shoved him, causing him to lose his balance and fall back. Stepping out of his shoes, Damon shucked everything but his underwear.

"Take off your pants," he demanded.

Marco rolled to his feet and stripped. Damon paused when Marco shed his boxers. He'd seen his friend's cock before plenty of times, but seeing it now felt different.

Marco grabbed him, hooked a leg behind his, and pushed Damon down on the bed, reversing their positions. Damon groaned as Marco grabbed his cock through his boxers.

"Did you think you were going to be in charge of this?" Marco's voice was low.

"You're damned right," Damon growled, licking his lips. Marco's palm was rubbing his cock, his thumb pressed against the head.

"We'll see." Marco grabbed Damon's boxers and pulled them off before joining him on the bed.

There was a shock of surprise as Marco's cock rested on Damon's hip. It was unfamiliar and alarming at first.

Needing to regain his equilibrium, Damon surged up, forcing Marco onto his back. Using his bulk to hold him down, Damon kissed him. Marco stroked his back before grabbing his ass and squeezing. It surprised Damon enough that Marco was able to roll him over and climb on top. He bit Damon's shoulder, his chest, while his fingers tugged on Damon's cock.

"Fuck," Damon moaned.

Marco danced his fingers over Damon's balls before dipping down to touch his anus.

Damon tossed Marco off and reversed their positions. When he pressed his finger against Marco's puckered entrance, the other man clenched his jaw, moaning.

"Wait."

Damon was shocked to hear Tasha's voice. He'd almost forgotten about her. Looking up, he was prepared to apologize to her, but she didn't seem angry.

"Give me your hand," she said.

Damon blinked in confusion. She pulled on his wrist, forcing him to stop touching Marco, who raised his head. "Tasha?"

She held up a glove and forced it on to Damon's left hand. She popped open a bottle of lube and poured some onto his fingers. "One finger to start, go slow and let his body adjust."

Damon was once again struck by this feeling that he would never really know her—she was a million different things. An hour ago, she'd been confessing her virgin status, and now she was a safe-sex referee and director.

Marco was distracted looking at her, so when Damon touched his anus, rubbing the lube against him, he jerked in surprise. That surprise quickly changed to a moan.

"Does that feel good?" Damon asked.

"Yes. But I want to fuck you."

Damon smiled. "That's too damn bad."

He thrust one finger into Marco's ass. It wasn't the first time he'd fingered someone's ass—it was a little embarrassing that he'd forgotten he needed lube until Tasha said something. But while he'd always carefully prepped his female lovers for anal sex, he'd been planning to simply fuck Marco.

"Damon," Marco moaned.

He added a second finger. Marco grabbed his head and brought it down for a brutal kiss. Damon started ramming his fingers into Marco's ass, enjoying the way Marco's body thrust down onto his hand.

The bed dipped and he broke the kiss to look at Tasha, who was sitting by Marco's head. She passed him a condom. Marco ripped it open and reached for Damon's cock.

Marco's touch was direct and forceful in a way a woman's never had been. Damon nearly came in his hand as Marco rolled the condom on.

"I need you now." Shoving Marco's legs open, Damon moved between them as Marco bent his knees. He'd never taken a woman anally face-to-face, but that's how he wanted Marco. He wanted to look into his blue eyes as he fucked him.

Guiding his cock with his hand, Damon positioned himself and then paused. Everything was about to change. Marco stroked his chest, thumbed his nipples and then drew him down for a kiss.

As their lips met, Damon thrust. Marco was tight, and he paused, letting the other man adjust.

"Fuck, that hurts," Marco growled.

Damon met his gaze and then pushed in deeper, forcing Marco to take him. To take him all. Marco gripped his shoulders, clinging to him.

When he was fully inside, Damon dropped his head, panting. "You okay?"

Marco's ass was tight around his cock, bringing him to the brink of coming.

"Yes. Fuck me."

Damon withdrew and then thrust in again. He started slow, conscious that he couldn't pound into Marco the way he wanted to—not at first. But soon Marco was groaning and demanded that he fuck harder, deeper. Damon dropped his body closer to Marco's, rubbing the other man's cock with his belly each time he thrust.

"I'm going to come," Damon said.

"Don't stop," Marco pleaded.

Damon reached between them and grabbed Marco's cock, playing with the head as he continued to fuck him. The pressure was mounting in his balls, and Damon couldn't hold back. He was slamming into Marco's ass, fucking him hard and rough while he tugged his cock.

He couldn't hold back any longer. Damon arched his back, holding himself deep inside Marco as he came. As he shuddered through his release, he stroked Marco's cock until he too was groaning and Damon felt wetness on his belly.

Damon released Marco's cock and braced himself on his elbows. They were both panting. His cock started to go soft and finally slipped from Marco's ass. Damon rolled to the side and stared at the canopy.

"Holy shit." It wasn't the most articulate or poetic thing

Damon had ever said post-sex, but it summed up his feelings. That had been the most intense sexual experience of his life.

Marco huffed out a laugh. "Yeah."

The bed dipped as Tasha knelt between them. She was biting her lip and her pupils were dilated. "I changed my mind. I want to be in the middle."

CHAPTER TEN

Damon leaned against the wall, watching as Marco seduced Tasha. They were sitting on the bed, Tasha leaning slightly away as if she still weren't sure she was ready. Damon had bowed out, not wanting to hurt or scare her. Plus, he needed some recovery time.

Marco eased the sweater off her shoulders, baring her arms. Though he'd seen Tasha essentially naked, the sight of even that little bit of flesh was tantalizing.

Damon took a step toward the bed. The movement startled Tasha, who twisted quickly away from Marco to look at him.

"Damon, why don't you get us some water?" Marco jerked his head to the side, indicating that Damon should give the two of them some space. Damon looked down at himself—apparently he didn't need as much recovery time as he thought. His cock was hard and his arm muscles clenched with the need to grab her. After the nearly brutal fucking he'd given Marco, Damon didn't trust himself with Tasha, and he was worried he would scare her.

He grabbed his pants and underwear off the floor and

pulled them on, hoping being half dressed would help him control himself. He went downstairs and grabbed their water glasses from the living room. Bracing his hands on the lip of the kitchen sink, he tried to get himself under control. All he could think about was Marco and Tasha together—the way they would look as their hands roamed over one another. Sticking his hand into his pocket, he pulled out his phone, planning to play a game until he'd calmed and recovered enough to join Marco and Tasha without being a brute. He played a quick game of Dots and then checked his email out of habit.

There was a message in his work account from a friend in the Chicago DA's office.

Thanks for the tip. Someone tried to sneak in to your friend's sister's room. Luckily the officer got them in time. Looks like she's into some bad stuff. When she's done detoxing we'll interview her about what's going on. Thinking she might be a mule.

Damon's blood chilled. Tasha had been right. Someone had tried to get to Jennie. If he hadn't started a process that got her police protection she might be dead.

He started to put his phone away—now wasn't the time to be checking emails. He needed to go back up to his spouses. Then he'd make love with both of them. Everything else could and would wait.

He tapped his thumb against the side of his phone. The cold feeling in his gut couldn't be ignored. Cursing himself, he opened his personal email.

Amid the junk was one titled *I'm sorry, please meet me*. It was from *Sandra S*.

Damon looked at the ceiling, knowing that in the bedroom upstairs Marco was wooing Tasha. That's what was important. He closed his eyes, not wanting to open the email and see what it said. But avoidance wasn't his way.

I'm so sorry I tried to blackmail you. I made a mistake—a

terrible one. Please meet me. I need your help. I'll give you back your phone, and I'll give you the video. Meet me tonight at midnight. Please.*

Damon read the email a second time, noticing that unlike the first time this correspondence was addressed to both him and Marco—their private email accounts. The address was in Chicago, and the email had been sent five hours ago. It was just past four now, meaning that if he was going to make that meeting he had under eight hours to get there.

Tasha touched his arm. Damon jumped and guiltily stuck his phone into his pocket. "Tasha, are you okay? Sorry," he said, forcing a smile. "I've got the water. Why are you down here?"

"What happened?" Her gaze searched his face.

"What are you talking about? Nothing happened. I was just taking a break so I didn't jump you."

"You're a terrible liar." Tasha turned and walked out of the kitchen. Damon stared at her. How the hell had she'd known something was up?

"What the hell?" Marco stormed in, his semi-erect cock bouncing.

"We have a problem," Damon said quietly. He read the email out loud.

"She sent it to me too?" Marco ran upstairs for his pants. When he came down he was looking at his phone. "We need to get back to Chicago. Don't tell Tasha."

"I think she suspects something is up. How did she know?"

"We were making out and then she just stopped, looked at the door and came down here. I thought she was coming to get you."

"Maybe she was, but she walked in on me reading this damned email."

They went in search of her and found her in a bedroom on the first floor. It was the girliest room Damon had ever seen.

The bed was covered with a pretty pastel quilt and there were paintings of flowers and sunsets on the walls. The headboard was white wicker, as was the vanity, which was covered in pretty glass figurines and perfume jars. The only jarring note was the black rolling suitcase open on the bed. Tasha was dressed in black slacks, an expensive-looking gold blouse and a knee-length fitted black coat. She went into the closet, pulled out a large tub, flipped open the top and selected a few items, tossing them into the suitcase.

"Tasha? What are you doing?" Marco asked.

"We need to go if we're going to make that meeting."

Damon cursed mentally. "What meeting?"

She paused, looked up and raised one brow.

He sighed. "How did you know?"

"I cloned your email. Marco's too. Everything you get I can see."

"Excuse me?" Damon frowned. "That's seriously illegal. And an invasion of my privacy."

Tasha zipped the suitcase. "I would say I'm sorry, but I'm not. I shouldn't have let myself get distracted. I was anticipating this, but after the whole marriage thing..." She looked irritated. "It was an amateur mistake."

She set the suitcase down and headed for the door. Damon blocked her exit. "You're staying here."

Tasha tipped her head to the side. "I know you're not serious."

"I am. Deadly. I meant what I said. We're going to protect you."

She smiled, stood on tiptoe and kissed his cheek. "That's sweet but stupid. It's my job to protect you."

"Damn it, Tasha." He held his position, refusing to let her pass.

"Move, Damon."

"No."

"You're not going to like this," she warned.

"Like what?"

She grabbed his thumb and jerked it back. His whole arm bent at a funny angle and he jumped to the side to relieve the pressure on reflex. Damon rubbed his hand and narrowed his eyes as she walked past. Marco held up his hands in a surrender pose and got out of her way.

She looked over her shoulder. "I need you ready in under ten minutes."

Damon looked at Marco—his friend, now his lover. Marco shrugged then headed upstairs. Eight minutes later, they were prepared to leave. Tasha took the key from Damon and they piled into the rental car.

SIX HOURS LATER, they were back in Marco's condo. Damon was feeling vaguely sick. They'd gotten up at four that morning in order to catch the first flight out of Boston. Most of the day had been spent traveling. The conversation they'd had in Tasha's house, followed by the sex, seemed like a dream.

Damon collapsed onto the couch. "Fuck, I'm tired. I feel like it's been a week since we were in Boston. Was that only yesterday?"

"No. It was this morning. We should eat something." Marco dropped down next to him.

Damon wrapped his arm around Marco's shoulders and kissed his temple. He did it without thinking, and it was only when he pulled back and saw Marco's surprised expression that he realized what he'd done.

He started to move his arm, but Marco caught his hand. "Don't," he said quietly. "It's nice."

TASHA WATCHED them cuddling on the couch and smiled sadly. It was nice to see them physically expressing the feelings she knew they had for each other. She reminded herself that this was what she wanted—to be part of a trinity in which the other two were the core of the relationship and she was an add on. That was safest for all of them. Part of her regretted urging them to form a sexual relationship that didn't involve her. She hadn't expected them to be so comfortable together. She hadn't wanted to be a sex-prop, existing only for them to have a way to touch each other. But in reality, it may have been her only way into their relationship. There was nothing she could do about it now—the hand was played.

She'd have to worry about it later. Right now she had less than three hours before the rendezvous. The email supposedly came from the missing redhead Sandra, but the trace she'd placed on the email had it coming from an IP in Singapore.

The address for the meeting was in the alley beside the BDSM club. There was no way that was a coincidence—clearly whoever was pulling the strings was going to use the fact she'd IDed Jennie and been to the club to his advantage. Tasha had no doubt this was a setup, but she couldn't see the end game yet and had no way to avoid it.

She'd been thinking about how best to approach tonight and decided they were going to go back in the same personas they'd used before. There might be some protection in the fact they would be noticed—Damon was probably barred from coming back, meaning there would be a scene when they tried to enter. Until she knew what was going on, Tasha wanted to give them the kind of protection eyewitnesses could provide.

She wasn't sure they'd realized where they were supposed

to rendezvous yet. Despite their race to the airport, neither man seemed overly concerned with what was supposed to happen.

Giving them space, she went to the spare bedroom and grabbed the gear they'd used before. She set out Damon's leather pants and vest on Marco's bed in the master bedroom and then selected a suit from his closet and laid that out too. She'd packed club-appropriate clothes for herself, including her favorite corset. Though it looked stiff it was actually fairly malleable, meaning she'd be able to bend and run if needed. And in the best spy tradition, there were pockets hidden along the boning that allowed her to tuck in a small knife, a high-powered audio recorder and a vial of LSD. It was nice to be prepared. She put on a long-sleeved high-neck fishnet shirt and then the corset. In contrast to her relatively covered top, she opted for black pleather panties that cut across the cheeks of her ass, leaving the lower curves exposed. She removed some of the heavy makeup she was wearing, letting the bruise on her face show, and then layered on gray shadow and black eyeliner.

Looking at herself in the mirror, she was satisfied with the mix of erotic and darkly feminine, but if she wanted to build on her prior persona and appearance she needed something else.

She left the bathroom, ran upstairs to the master bedroom and pulled the belt from Damon's leather pants. As she came down, she called to the guys to get ready. Tasha retreated to the guest bathroom, turned on the shower and waited until she heard their footsteps pass. The noise of the water would help cover what she was about to do. Bending at the waist, Tasha braced one hand on the wall. Looking over her shoulder in the mirror, she raised the belt.

MARCO FOLLOWED Damon into the master bedroom. Tasha was in the shower on the first floor. He hadn't realized how late it was. They needed to leave and quickly.

"Shit," Damon muttered when he saw what was out on the bed. "I was just thinking it was wifely of her to pick out our clothes. Not these clothes."

"What the hell?" Marco looked at the leather outfit Damon was meant to wear.

"Did you check the address where we're supposed to meet?" Damon asked him.

"No."

"I did. It looks like it's an alley behind the club."

"We can't go back there. They kicked you out."

"I know. Maybe we didn't tell Tasha that."

"Why would we need to go into the club anyway if we're meeting behind it?"

"I don't know."

"I'll ask her. You should get dressed just in case."

"Takes me twenty minutes to get into the damned pants." Damon's mutterings faded as Marco went downstairs to the guest bath.

As he approached the door, he heard an odd noise—almost like a slapping sound.

"Tasha?" He approached the door slowly. Having never lived with a girlfriend, he had no idea what she might be doing in there.

He heard the slap again, this time followed by a soft cry. The sound was so quiet he almost didn't hear it over the noise of the shower.

"Tasha." Heart beating fast, he threw the door open.

In the instant before she realized he was there, he saw her face—her eyes were squeezed shut, her teeth gritted. She was dressed—from the hips up. Her legs and the lower curve of her ass cheeks were naked. She held a belt in her right hand and was whipping herself with it. Her skin was crisscrossed with faint red welts and lines.

Her face smoothed out as she realized he'd opened the door. "You're not dressed."

Marco was too shocked to say anything—both from what she was doing and by how easily she'd masked her pain.

"Tasha." His voice was hoarse. "Beautiful, what are you doing?"

"What I need to." She examined her reflection in the mirror. "Almost done. Please close the door."

"What? No." Marco grabbed the belt and yanked it out of her grasp.

"What's going on?" Damon, dressed in the same leather outfit as before, joined Marco. He looked at Tasha and then cursed. "Damn it, Tasha."

"Why are you upset? I didn't ask either of you to help me since that was clearly a problem last time." She motioned to her face.

"Why are you hurting yourself?" Marco asked.

"Because, just like last time, we want to attract attention."

"And why does that mean you have to be hurt? You're more than this—than sex and violence." Marco was struggling to keep from yelling.

She let out a little laugh. "Sex and violence? The history of mankind is littered with women being the objects of sex and violence. I hate that and I know I'm doing nothing to change it. I use it. I make myself a sex object. I allowed violence to be done to me and do it to others. I'm not trying to make a political point or do social justice work. My job is to be and play with the darkest parts of mankind. And I do it so that people like you can be good.

"I do it so you, Damon, will sit on the federal bench and

make sure there is justice. I do it so you, Marco, will make music that brings people joy. I understand and I appreciate that you want to protect me, but you have to let me do this. You have to let me be who I am."

She held out her hand. "Now give me back the belt. I will be done in a few minutes. Then we'll go."

Marco passed the belt back to Damon, who chucked it away. It thumped on the floor.

"No." Marco took two steps, caught a hold of Tasha's arms and turned her to face him. "You were those things, and you are an amazing, fascinating woman. But now you're more than the darkness. You are ours. Our wife."

She shook her head. "You have each other."

"Yes," Marco said. "We have each other, and we also have you. We all have each other. If we'd had more time this afternoon, we would have shown you exactly how much you are ours."

"I thought you might use me to have sex," she admitted. "Neither of you seemed like you would be up for male intercourse. But you're fine by yourselves. You don't really need me."

"You think we should have been using you in order to have sex with each other?" Damon sounded outraged.

Tasha shook her head. "I shouldn't have started this conversation. We really don't have time. We're leaving."

But Marco wasn't ready to walk away. He needed her to know how much he cared about her. "Do you understand I hate seeing you in pain? I don't care if you want to parade around naked in front of a bunch of people. I don't own you. Neither of us does, and we absolutely respect your right over your own body. But as your husbands, we have the right to stop you from hurting yourself. The same way you have a right to protect us."

"I know it must be hard to understand," she said. "But this is normal for me. This is me prepping to go to work."

"You never have to do this again." Damon's voice was thick with conviction. "You don't ever have to be someone or do something you don't want to in order to protect or help someone else. I don't care what we have to do to make that a reality. I'll find a way to make sure you never have to do this again."

Marco nodded in agreement. "Let's walk away. We'll find a way to pay the blackmail. We won't go to the meeting. We'll just stay here. Stay here and have amazing sex."

Tasha only shook her head. "There's more at stake and more going on than you know."

"Then tell us."

"I can't. We need to go. It's getting late." She looked in the mirror at her ass and sighed. "The marks aren't dark enough to show up in the dim light." She pulled her hair up into a ponytail. "I'll figure it out in the car."

Marco wanted to grab Tasha and shake her until she listened to him. He felt as if they'd lost her. The vulnerable girl she had been in that pretty yellow farmhouse was gone. Now she was the capable, slightly aloof woman who'd first shown up in his condo. He had to content himself with the idea that once tonight was over they would have plenty of time to work on their relationship. He was going to marry that woman, marry her at the same time he married his best friend. And nothing was going to stand in his way.

"They're not going to let us back in." Damon pulled the door of the limo closed after he got in.

"They will." Tasha stripped off the jacket she put on to

cover up her outfit while they walked out of the building. "There was a noticeable upswing in their bookings and reservations after we were there. You did what they're not allowed to do—really beat someone."

"There goes my faith in humanity. It's good for business having someone beating up women?"

"In a BDSM club it can be."

"How do you know about their bookings?"

"I've been monitoring their systems remotely."

Damon muttered something that might have been *felony*.

Tasha pulled items from the big bag she'd carried to the car. She handed a mask to each of them and then took out the collar, cuffs and two leashes. It was amazing to her what a difference a few days made. Amazing how much the three of them had been through since the last time they had been in this limo. That night Damon had been pragmatic and cold, willing to do what was necessary. But now she'd seen what was underneath that cold exterior. And Marco, who'd been so protective when they were in Las Vegas, was now even more so, and yet she knew he was angry with her. She could feel his frustration.

"Here, let me help you." Damon held out his hand, reaching for the collar.

"No. I'll do it." Marco moved to sit next to Tasha, taking the leather restraints from the seat. She slipped onto her knees in front of him. Her ass and thighs hurt from the belting she'd given them. It had been a wasted effort, unfortunately.

Holding out her arms, she watched as Marco wrapped the cuffs around her wrists. As he fastened each buckle her breathing grew heavy. Her nipples tightened into points inside the corset, and her pussy throbbed. Now that she knew them, now that she'd kissed them and watched them touch and kiss each other, she was having trouble thinking of this as an op and distancing herself from the physical reality of being dressed as, and acting like, their submissive.

Marco picked up the collar.

"Give me a second." Tasha sat back licking her lips.

Damon shifted, moving closer to them. "Tasha?"

"I just need a second to remember the plan, to remind myself what's happening here." She felt like she was babbling.

Marco hooked his finger under her chin and tipped her face so he could look at her. "Tasha, beautiful, do you like this? I mean really like it?"

She licked her lips. Part of her wanted to lie, but a bigger part of her wanted to tell them her desires...and see what they'd do with that information. "I've always understood the sexual appeal of games like this," she said haltingly. "But danger or the need to extract information has always distracted me and kept me from actually engaging on a real emotional and physical level."

A slow smile worked its way across Marco's face. The collar of his shirt was open, the tie dangling around his neck. His dark hair fell over his forehead, and in the recessed lights of the limo the planes of his face were smooth and strong. "So you're saying that for the first time in your life you're getting to actually enjoy some bondage play."

She looked away from his handsome, sexy face. "I need to stay focused. I don't have time to be distracted. Don't distract me."

Marco dipped his head and kissed her briefly. "Fine. I won't distract you. But we are coming back to this topic later. I assumed since you learned all of this in a rather horrifying way that any sex games or kinks would always be disgusting to you."

"No, not disgusting." Tasha sat forward and bent her head, shivering as Marco fastened the collar around her neck. When he was done, he kissed her again, his lips lingering on hers.

Then Damon was at her back. He kissed the tops of her shoulders through the holes in the fishnet, raised her hands and kissed her palms before lacing their fingers together.

"We don't have time for this." She tried to be strong when she said it, but her words were breathy.

Marco pulled back. "Unfortunately, I know you're right."

"What's the plan?" Damon released her. "Just so you know, I won't hit you again."

"That's what I was trying to avoid by doing the whipping myself at home. What we want is to get in there and make sure everyone sees us."

"But we need to get out of there to get to the rendezvous spot."

"And we will, but I want both of you to have alibis in case anything happens. My plan was for the two of you to show off how you punished me for disobeying last time. Then you'd invite a few select people from the audience to join us in a private room to see more punishment."

"I hate everything about this plan." Damon said.

Tasha touched his hand. "I knew you would. But this time you aren't actually going to do anything. Or at least you weren't going to have to before. Now if no one can see the marks, we might have a problem. There's my face, but only a few people will find that alluring, while a nicely beaten ass will have more widespread appeal."

"This is a weird conversation." Damon ran his hands though his hair.

"What's the point of getting some other people in a private room with us?" Marco asked.

"We're going to drug them. We'll be seen entering the room with them and seen leaving the room with them an hour later. During that time, we will have snuck out for the rendezvous."

"Drug them?" Damon sighed. "This is so very, very illegal."

"Like I said, there's no law here."

"I still don't see why you have to be marked up for this plan to work," Marco said.

"Most of these people in the club are probably normal, with nine-to-five jobs and the kind of lives that mean they can't, even if they wanted to, get beat with the belts so hard that they're bruised. Damon is being set apart as a man who can and will do things most of them only get to talk or think about."

"So what now?" Damon asked. "Am I going to spank you with the belt again?"

"That was play, and we both know it—sound and fury. That spanking was barely better than what their performers are doing."

His lips thinned. "I'll have to hit you again."

"No, I won't make you do that." Tasha touched his knee. "I saw how much it upset you."

"You're going to get someone else to do it, aren't you?" Marco asked.

"There are other things we could do to attract attention," Tasha said. "But punishment is actually a bit easier and less revealing than one of you fucking me in the middle of the room or having to strip and pose." Looking at their distressed expressions, Tasha mentally rearranged her plan. "Okay, I'll think of something else. They had a few different devices that we could ask to use. That might be enough, if we play it as if you're forcing me into it." She didn't like the idea of being in heavy bondage that would take time to get out of.

"No. This is my fault. I didn't trust you and I should have." Marco was looking at her, his blue eyes nearly black in the shadows. "Damon, give me your belt." The air in the limo thickened. Tasha, who still knelt on the floor between them, looked from one man to another. In the dim, enclosed space they were large and powerful—threatening and enticing.

"Tasha," Marco said. "I want to say that I'll protect you. I want to say that you'll never have to be hurt again. But I'm not going to say those things if all I'm doing is forcing you to trade one kind of pain for another."

Tasha sighed in a combination of relief and sadness that she'd forced them to see the world the way she did. Where blood and bruises were actually easier than emotional vulnerability.

Damon's jaw was clenched, but he took off the belt, pulling it through the loops and passing it to Marco. Tasha started to climb onto Marco's lap but Damon stopped her and pulled her back against his chest.

"There's no reason this has to be all pain," he said. "Let's pretend that you really are our submissive, and that a spanking might not just be punishment."

Tasha held her breath as Damon tangled his fingers in her hair and turned her face to his. He captured her lips in his soft, deep kiss. He stroked her breasts. Her nipples were pebbled against the satiny material of the inside of the corset. Each breath was its own pleasure.

Marco slid to his knees in front of her. He found the edge of her panties and tugged them down little by little until they tangled around her ankles.

CHAPTER ELEVEN

When he pulled her panties off and pressed her legs open, Tasha lifted her hips. She felt wanton—half-mad with desire. Though they were headed into danger, all she could think about was their hands on her needy body. Soon Marco would bend her over his lap and take the belt to her, hitting her hard enough to leave marks that would be visible in the dim lights of the club. Instead of making her feel afraid or resigned, the idea was driving her arousal higher, pushing her to the brink of a dark well of sexual need she'd never let herself fall into. For the first time in her life, she was engaging in sexual contact with people who cared about her. It was freeing.

They were not assets to be cultivated, they were not foreign intelligence agents to be seduced or drugged. They were not teachers or students entering her life to further her training or allow her to pass on what she knew. They were her husbands, they were her partners, and they were about to be her lovers.

Marco kneaded the insides of her thighs, his thumbs

grazing her pussy. "Have you ever had a man's lips here?" he asked.

"Yes. I wasn't a saint." She gasped as he stroked her.

Marco chuckled while Damon kissed the spot under her ear just above the collar. Marco pressed two fingers between her outer labia, stroking up and down, with each pass brushing her clit. Tasha's breath was coming fast. It seemed crazy that she was so aroused so quickly, and yet she knew it wouldn't take much to push her over the edge. Maybe it was because she'd wanted them since she met them, or maybe it was because she knew that with these men, for the first time in her life, sex would come without strings attached.

Damon captured her lips in another kiss as Marco dipped his head to her pussy. Tasha screamed, her whole body tensing, her hips lifting, as Marco's tongue pressed into her, finding and stroking her clit. He dipped his fingers lower, sliding one into her, giving her the little bit of penetration that she'd only ever felt with fingers and toys. She wanted it to be his cock. Wanted to feel him thrusting into her as Damon kissed her. Wanted to feel Damon behind her, his cock sliding into her ass as Marco took her from the front.

She'd told them she was afraid of being in the middle sexually, and that was true. She was afraid. But she was also painfully, epically aroused by the idea. This was only a taste, a preview of what it would be like when they weren't rushed and in the back of a car. And even this had her teetering on the brink of an orgasm so powerful she feared she would never recover from it.

Marco added a second finger, stretching her open. He worked her clit with his tongue, first circling the outside with just enough stimulation to keep her on the edge but not enough to push her over. Then he would nip her lightly, a little dart of pain amid all the pleasure. But it was what she wanted, what she needed. The best part was the long, slow strokes of his tongue. Every nerve ending was stimulated, every bit of her felt his touch.

She was biting and sucking on Damon's tongue. She unashamedly dug fingers into Marco's hair, forcing his face tighter against her sex. She grabbed Damon's hand and squeezed it against her breasts, trying to force his fingers under the top of her corset. He understood her need and tugged it down enough to expose her nipples, then plucked the tight buds through the holes in the fishnet. When she broke from the kiss and pressed her face into his neck, begging them both for more, whimpering in her need, Damon began to pinch, twist and roll her nipples while Marco focused on licking her up and down in a steady, incessant rhythm.

Tasha moaned and thrashed, ready to feel the pleasure that crawled inside her break, splintering apart into a million little shards of happy bright light. But just when she was there, Marco pulled back.

"No," she growled, grabbing for him. Before she realized what was happening Marco had taken a seat and Damon was lifting her, settling her face down over Marco's lap. She'd forgotten what had started this, forgotten what she'd asked them to do. Her ass was naked and exposed, completely at Marco's mercy.

Damon knelt, brushing her hair gently back from her face. "Tell us what you need."

"I've never done this before," Marco said.

"Four or five hits should be enough," she said, cheek against the seat. "They need to be hard enough that they'll still be red when we get there and hopefully darken up over the next hour."

Damon leaned in and kissed her. He nipped her lower lip and sucked it into his mouth, laving it with his tongue. The denied orgasm was still there, rolling and bubbling in her belly. Tasha wanted to come, needed to orgasm more than she could ever remember.

Damon kept kissing her and slid his hand between her body and the seat to find her nipple, to pinch and twist it. That sent little darts of pleasure down into her pussy.

Crack.

Tasha jerked in surprise when the first blow landed against her butt. It hurt where it overlapped with her earlier attempts, but she knew it wasn't hard enough to leave a mark.

"Harder," she begged when Damon broke the kiss. "It has to be harder."

Crack. This one landed at the upper part of her thighs, the blow sending fissures of pain up and down her back. She jerked her mouth away from Damon so she wouldn't bite him as she clenched her teeth.

"I hurt you." Marco's voice was rough, his distress evident.

"Yes, yes," she whispered. "Do it again."

In her heightened state of arousal, the pain was more than just pain—it was sensation, it was feeling. When the third blow fell, it jiggled her ass. For a moment she thought that would be it, that would be what made her come.

"Hold on a second." Damon slid one of her legs off the seat and slipped his fingers into her pussy, sliding from the entrance of her body to her clit, stroking and rubbing her. The touch pushed her back toward that brink of orgasm, but before she could go over, Damon withdrew his hand and forced her leg back up onto the seat.

Crack.

This time Tasha screamed. It was as much in frustration as in pain.

"Do you want to come?" Damon squeezed her nipple.

"Yes, yes, please." Tasha didn't care she was begging, didn't care that it was artless begging, or that everything she was doing was unplanned. In this moment, she didn't care about them, didn't care if when they looked at her they saw the ultimate object of their desires, which had always been her goal before. She was, for the first time, totally and completely selfish. It was glorious.

Crack. The blow landed at the ultra-soft skin where the top of her thighs met her ass. Tasha screamed and kicked, her legs sliding off the seat. Damon caught her, pulled her down and turned her so she lay flat on the floor of the limo.

He grabbed her cuffs and forced her hands above her head as his teeth closed over her nipple, holding it tight as he sucked. Marco tossed the belt aside and came down on his knees before her, forcing her legs open. Cupping her hips in his hands, he lifted her to his mouth and focused his lips and tongue on her clit.

The burning pain from her beaten ass and the little sharp darts of pain at her nipples were a stark contrast to the deep, rolling pleasure of Marco's tongue on her clit. She wanted more. She wanted this to go on forever, and yet she wanted them to give her what she craved, what she desired, right now.

She realized she would never have enough of them. There would never be enough touches, enough kisses. Enough pain, enough pleasure.

Marco shifted, and with his tongue still on her clit, he thrust two fingers into her pussy. That was it. Tasha pressed her head back and screamed in pleasure as she came, her body tense and taut as a metal wire. It seemed to go on forever—great rolling swoops of pleasure cascading through her. Her toes curled, hands fisted. She was gasping their names, begging them to never stop.

And they didn't stop. Hands, lips and teeth all continued to caress her, prolonging the orgasm to the point of sensory and nerve overload. Finally, her body shuddered to a stop, and she tugged free of Marco's restraining hold and pushed their heads away. Lying on the floor half-naked and sprawled open before them, Tasha couldn't think of anything to say. As if they realized that, Marco and Damon both helped her onto the seat and cradled her against their bodies the way they had on the couch in her home earlier that day.

There were things she wanted to say and things she didn't want to ever have to say. But the limo glided to a halt and she looked out the window. The club. It was time to go.

"Thank you," she whispered.

Damon handed her panties, which she tugged on, hissing as the material slid over her ass.

"Did I hurt you?" Marco asked. "I got... Fuck. I got a little enthusiastic."

"Yes, you did. Thank you." Tasha smiled at him. "That was, by far, the best spanking I've ever had."

"Next time we'll do it without the belt, just you over my knee." His eyes were dark and she realized the men were both seriously aroused. She liked that playing with her brought them to that point.

"I think next time I'll spank you," she teased. "Or maybe you can spank Damon?" She felt slightly giddy from the pleasure that still rippled through her. Now that the orgasm itself was fading, she was aware of each of the stripes Marco had laid on her. Even that pain was strangely pleasant, as if absence of the danger that had in the past accompanied something like this had stripped the physical pain of any emotional impact.

"Fat, fucking chance." Damon grabbed his mask and one of the leashes. "Let's do this. The sooner we get it over with the sooner we can go home and fuck."

MARCO LOOKED AT TASHA. He wanted to throw his jacket over her to cover her so no one else could see what he most definitely was starting to think of as his. Guilt warred with a strange sort of pride as he looked at the marks on her thighs and butt. He hated he'd done that to her, and yet he felt a primal satisfaction. He'd marked his woman. He'd given her pleasure so intense it had masked pain. The only thing that could've made it better was if he'd been fucking her, his cock sliding in and out of her.

Part of him was aware of the reality that when he was no longer so painfully aroused he would probably be horrified. The atmosphere and intimacy of the limo had pushed him into doing something he would never do normally. He'd hit her with that belt—and he'd hit her hard.

Marco now understood the guilt that had racked Damon. This time, Marco had the benefit of being able to combine pleasure with pain, which Damon hadn't been able to do.

Tasha was right. When they arrived, the bouncer tried to stop them from entering, but after radioing in who was at the door, Demario showed up. The manager lectured them but still let them in. As they crossed the room, Marco heard people whispering about them, commenting on Tasha's ass and the evidence of her punishment. They were ushered to a table near the center of the room and then told that there was no one using the main stage right now.

It wasn't exactly an invitation, but when a bottle of top-shelf whiskey showed up at their table, compliments of the management, it was all too apparent that Demario hoped Damon would do something dangerous.

And Damon was more than happy to oblige. He ordered Tasha up onto the stage and strapped her to the St. Andrews Cross that was there. In the spotlight, the marks on her ass were all too apparent—angry red against the pale tones of her flesh.

Marco took another sip of whiskey. At least his arousal had died. Now that they were here, he was able to focus on their mission. He was tense and constantly looking around for the redhead they'd fucked that night at the party. He didn't expect to see her, but it gave him something to do until they were supposed to meet her in the alley.

"Time," Damon muttered. He was sitting, chair turned so he was looking at Tasha. "We need to hurry up."

"You get up onstage. I'll figure out who we're going to invite into a private room." Marco shifted, scanning the crowd that pressed in closer around them the instant Damon got up next to Tasha. She put on a good show, thrashing and whimpering when she saw him. For his part, Damon very deliberately removed his belt, which had been off more than it had been on. He folded it in his hand and slapped it against his leg, the snapping sound loud even with the annoying music. Each time he did it, Tasha whimpered and jerked, the chains that connected her cuffs to the cross clanking.

Her fear was arousing. It was a terrible thing to think, a terrible thing to feel—that a woman's suffering would inspire arousal. But that was what Marco felt twinges of, and that's what he saw on the faces of the men in the crowd. When Damon stroked her back and ass with the back of his hand, whimpers turned to moans. Maybe that was why it was arousing—because Tasha made the line between fear and desire, arousal and pain, seem like a very thin thing.

"Have you learned your lesson?" Damon said loud enough that the crowd could hear. His mask rendered him anonymous and his muscled arms seemed massive compared to her slender limbs.

Marco had very little doubt he could ask anyone in the crowd to join them and they would agree. But one little group caught his eye. It was three young people. They looked barely old enough to be in the club. The girl was dressed in a mix of Goth and latex with a ridiculous amount of black eyeliner on. Her male companions had slightly less black eyeliner and were both dressed in ways that Marco assumed were meant to be intimidating. One wore high boots with spikes. His chest was bare except for a crisscross of leather straps. The second man wore a long coat and sunglasses, which was completely ridiculous considering how dark and hot it was in the club. He looked vaguely like a movie vampire. He hadn't filled out yet, and though he had height, he seemed gangly rather than intimidating.

Marco pointed at them and then curled his finger, beckoning them over. They looked startled, but after a minute they pushed through the crowd and came to where he was sitting. Without a word, he motioned to the chairs around their table.

"Hello, Sir," the girl said a little too brightly. She cleared her throat and lowered her voice. "Hello, Sir."

"Name?" Marco kept his voice low, and if he were completely honest he would admit that he was enjoying playing the mysterious man.

"My name is Dark Diamond." She dropped her chin and tried to look seductive.

"And them?" Marco indicated the boys with a flick of his finger.

The one wearing the straps instead of a shirt cleared his throat and then attempted to growl out his name. "Master Blackwolf."

"And you?" He pointed to the last man.

"Bane."

Marco was intensely proud of himself for not laughing at their chosen monikers. "Do you enjoy what my friend is doing to his slave?"

Their attention jumped from Marco to the stage where

Damon was running his hand over Tasha's ass and legs. She was thrashing and crying out, promising him she'd be a good girl.

"She was punished." The way the boy who called himself Master Blackwolf said it, with utter relish, raised Marco's hackles.

He didn't let that show. "Yes, she was disobedient. My friend dealt with her accordingly."

"I think we read about you online," Bane said.

"That's what we wanted to come and see," Dark Diamond added.

"Then perhaps you'll join us to see the conclusion of the slave's punishment." Marco raised his hand and summoned over Demario. "We need privacy."

After a whispered conversation with the club manager, Marco climbed to his feet, the three wannabes in tow. He met Damon's eye and jerked his head, picking up the bottle of whiskey as they left the table. Damon quickly released Tasha from the St. Andrew's cross. He hooked the leash to the ring in front of her collar and led her off stage. She dropped to her knees and crawled after them. Every eye was on her as Marco guided the little party into a back room and closed the door firmly behind them.

TASHA STARTED WHIMPERING as she pressed her hands against her waist. "Please, Master, I'll be a good girl." She fished the vial of LSD out of its secret pocket and palmed it. She reached up and rested her hands against Damon's belly, making sure he felt that she was holding something. "One drop," she breathed.

He put his hands over hers, took the vial and then pushed

her arms away. "Enough," he barked, winking at her. "You deserve punishment for saying no."

"Shall I pour drinks?" Marco asked.

"No, I'll do it."

Tasha watched as Damon carefully poured out five glasses, his body hiding what he was doing from their guests, but she saw him put a single drop from the vial into each of the first three glasses, which he gave to the people Marco had selected.

"So we gonna fuck her?" The boy wearing a trench coat and sunglasses asked Damon.

"No, I want to see her get punished." The other boy was practically vibrating in his eagerness to see her abused. "Where are you going to beat her? Her tits? Her pussy?"

Tasha fought to hold back a disgusted sneer. From the way Damon and Marco tensed, she had a feeling they were also less than pleased. It was nice to know they were upset on her behalf. In another time, if she were on this op with other people, she might have had to let one of those boys beat her. Tonight she wouldn't. That felt good.

"Drink." Damon raised his glass and downed it in one swallow. After looking at each other, the two boys and the girl did the same. It would take anywhere from twenty minutes to a half hour for the drug to kick in. The vial held liquid LSD diluted in alcohol. It would be enough to have them seeing things, but not enough to have them jumping off a building.

Marco caught her eye and Tasha subtly flashed two fingers. He seemed to understand her signal.

"Tell us about yourselves," Marco said, crossing his legs.

"What about her?" the one in sunglasses whined.

"You dare to criticize what I do with my property?" Damon crossed his arms, the muscles of his biceps swelling. "I don't like them," he growled at Marco.

"Now, now, my friend. They're young."

Damon snorted. "They presume to question my methods. They demand to see my slave punished. They make demands of me? As if I were their slave?"

"I'm sure they didn't mean that." Marco swirled the liquid in his glass. "Did you?"

Tasha bit the inside of her cheek to keep from laughing. Marco and Damon were enjoying this. She could see it in the way their lips would occasionally twitch, hear it in their voices and their ridiculous dialogue.

The newcomers were stammering, trying and failing to seem like they knew what was going on. When their babbling quieted for a moment, Tasha rose to her feet, keeping her head bowed.

"I'll get your bag, Master," she murmured.

There was a slight pause and then Damon answered. "Good, slave."

Rather than going back into the club, Tasha slipped out into the back hall. She had a fairly good idea of the layout of the private areas of the club from her prior visit. Using the same exit door she had before, she let herself out and used a dumpster and a ledge to climb onto the roof. The address given for the rendezvous actually belonged to a shipping company whose front door was in the alley at the side of the club. She ran across the roof to get to that side and then lay down and examined the meeting location.

Unlike the dark, dumpster-filled alley she'd emerged into, this one was large, clean and well lit. It dead-ended into a shipping and receiving bay. There were at least three security cameras covering the entire space.

Tasha pulled back, closing her eyes so she could think. She was only going to get one chance to prevent whatever was going on—meaning that if she guessed wrong she may put Marco and Damon in very real danger. She had only a vague idea of the motivation for this attack on Marco and Damon, and by extension the Trinity Masters. She was being forced to guess not only what cards the other player held, but also what game they were playing. But Tasha was a very good guesser.

Checking the alley one last time, she made her way back across the roof. Her stomach was knotted with anxiety—the stakes were higher than they ever had been before. She wasn't just protecting a member of the Trinity Masters, she was fighting for her future. If she was right about what was going on, they had only a matter of hours to make sure this whole thing didn't go to hell.

CHAPTER TWELVE

"What did you give them?" Marco asked, pushing his mask up.

The three people they'd lured into the private room with promises of a show were now slumped in their chairs. Their eyes were open, and the boy in the trenchcoat was muttering to himself.

"I have no idea. I really hope I didn't just kill them."

"Do you think I would have given you poison?" Tasha asked.

Damon jumped. "Stop doing that."

"What?" She came to stand between them, looking down at their victims.

"Sneaking up on us."

"I don't sneak up on you."

"You're like a damned ninja," Damon muttered. Marco laughed.

"You didn't kill them. It's acid. LSD. They're having a great time."

"Acid. I gave them acid." Damon ran a hand through his hair. "Is there any point in my saying how illegal that is?"

"No," Tasha and Marco said at the same time.

"You need to go." Tasha led them out though the door she'd used and into an alley. "Leave your masks here. And Damon, leave the vest, wear Marco's jacket."

"No disguises?" he asked.

"No." Tasha was frowning, and for the first time she looked worried. "I don't want you on video looking like you're sneaking around."

"Video?" Damon looked at Marco. "Tasha, what's going on?"

"Hurry." She wrapped their masks up in Damon's vest. "Go around the front of the building, past the entrance. The meeting place is in the alley on the other side. You'll see it—there's a door for a shipping company. That's the address she gave."

"Where are you going to be?"

"I'll have eyes on you." Tasha climbed onto a dumpster, leapt and grabbed a second-floor window ledge and pulled herself up. In less than thirty seconds, she was on the roof.

"Ninja," Marco agreed.

"Come on." Damon shrugged on Marco's jacket, which was too tight and felt strange without a shirt. Following her directions, they passed the entrance to the club. The bouncer didn't even look at them, nor did the people waiting in the velvet rope line.

Damon's shoulders were tense and his heart was pounding as they stepped off the sidewalk into the wide, clean alleyway.

There was no one there.

Marco checked his watch. "Ten minutes."

At five past twelve Damon was getting irritated. He hated waiting, hated not knowing. "Where the hell is she?"

Marco was leaning against the wall. He yawned and then shrugged. Movement at the mouth of the alley caught Damon's eye. He looked over to see a thin woman with long dark hair stumbling toward them.

"Marco," he said.

Marco straightened and then came to stand beside him, shoulder to shoulder.

The woman was humming to herself. When she looked up, Damon scanned her face. She wasn't the redhead they'd fucked in the video. The girl was clearly at least part Asian with dark slanted eyes. Hair color could change, but not the shape of the face.

Disappointment rolled through Damon.

"Hey, boys," she said, stopping in front of them. "Do you want to party?"

"Do you have his phone?" Damon asked her uncertainly.

"Phone?"

"Why are you here?" he asked. "Where's Sandra?"

"I can be Sandra, muscles." She leaned into him.

Damon jerked back and pushed her away. She grabbed his hair and yanked it—hard.

"What the hell?" Marco pushed her back, getting between Damon and the woman. She snatched Marco's tie and pulled it off his neck.

"What's this for, huh? Wanna tie me up?"

"You need to leave," Marco said, backing up.

"Fine." She held up her hands. Her voice went cold. "Then you'll never know who's setting you up." The facade of drunk party girl was gone. The brunette turned on her heel and sprinted out of the alley.

Damon started to run after her when Tasha's voice stopped him in his tracks.

"It's a trap."

He looked up at the roof but couldn't see her.

"Stay there and don't move," she said. He could just barely hear her. "Actually, lean against that wall and start making out."

Damon ran his hands through his hair—his whole body was thrumming with the need to chase that woman and find out what the hell was going on.

"Don't." Marco wrapped an arm around him. "Trust Tasha."

"I want this over."

"I know, me too." Marco started backing Damon towards the wall beside the door of the shipping company. "Don't think about it."

"How the hell am I supposed to do that?"

"I'll help you." Marco's hips settled against Damon's and he unbuttoned the too-tight coat, spreading it open so he could stroke Damon's chest.

Leaning his head back against the bricks, Damon let Marco's touch cool the anger and frustration that filled him, replacing it with a different kind of heat. He ground his hips against Marco's, the tight pants cutting into his erection.

Marco's lips closed over his. Damon cupped his head, deepening the kiss. Marco tasted like whiskey.

When they parted to take a breath, Marco cupped Damon's neck. "Next time I'm fucking you."

"We'll see." Damon grinned. "I liked seeing you eat out Tasha."

"And I liked seeing you hold her down while I did it."

They came together, lips fused, hands roaming, grabbing. The touches increasingly more erotic and demanding.

Marco pulled back, rubbing his shoulder.

"You okay?" Damon asked.

"Something just hit me."

Damon looked at the roof. He could just barely see Tasha standing there, beckoning them.

"Time to go." He looped his arm around Marco. They circled the building and returned to the door in the dark alley. Tasha was there and handed back their masks and Damon's vest.

"What's going on?" Damon asked as he switched Marco's summer-weight wool coat for the heavy leather vest.

Tasha only shook her head. She looked worried, which set alarm bells off in Damon's mind.

"We need to make sure we're remembered." She fiddled with the door and then opened it. "After we deal with the three we've got in there, we need to go back into the main room and stay until closing."

Damon stopped her once they were all inside. "Tasha, what's going on? You need to tell us."

He could barely see her in the lightless hall. Marco crowded against him to hear her reply.

"You're being set up," she said. "For what, I'm not sure. I suspect..." She shook her head. "There's no point in speculating. What we need are alibis. Damon, you're the one who's concerned about keeping things legal—well, now is the time to think about creating reasonable doubt. That's what we're doing."

Damon was cold and felt vaguely sick. "Fuck," he whispered.

Tasha touched his cheek and then Marco's. "Don't worry. I'll make sure you're safe. All I need you to do right now is forget what I just said and go back to playing the mysterious, sexy Masters."

"Maybe we should go to the DA," Damon said.

Tasha pressed herself against him. "Why don't we stay

here?" she whispered softly. "Why don't we stay here and have fun. You were enjoying it. I know you were."

Damon's cock swelled. "Tasha, stop, you're making it hard to think logically."

"Good." She drew Marco over so that Damon was between them—Tasha at his front, Marco at his back. There were breasts against his chest and a cock against his ass.

"Marco? Will you stay and play? You haven't gotten a turn to be my Master. Do you want that?"

Damon felt Marco's cock jump at her words.

"I know she's playing us," Marco said. "But I don't care."

Damon huffed out a laugh. Giving in, he grabbed the ring in Tasha's collar and jerked her onto her toes. "You are very dangerous," he whispered against her lips.

"Yes, yes, I am."

AN HOUR AND A HALF LATER, Tasha moaned loudly as Marco freed her from the St. Andrew's cross. She was only half-acting as she clung to him. Her legs were stiff from being stuck in one position for so long, and her hands throbbed as she dropped them to her sides.

She eased herself to her knees. Marco's hand on her head made it seem like he was forcing her down. The crowd was being dispersed by the bouncers, and the house lights were coming on. It was two a.m. and the club was closed.

Master Blackwolf, Black Diamond and Bane were preening as they stood from their seats of honor close to the stage. They'd spent the last hour telling anyone who came close to them that they'd helped punish her. They were still tripping on acid, but she doubted they'd question Marco's statement to them—that good whiskey and kinky sex had given them that high.

As they'd emerged from the first flush of acid, she'd positioned herself over their laps or on her knees in front of them and cried and begged for them to stop. That was all it had taken for their imaginations to fill in the blanks. She'd heard them telling a variety of stories about what they'd done to her—each more graphic and horrifying than the last. Black Diamond's story included an elaborate setup where she was whipping Tasha while Marco fucked her.

Marco's groans indicated he'd heard the girl's fantasy story.

Tasha had gone back onto the St. Andrew's cross as soon as they'd left the private room. Damon had helped her rip the fishnet shirt and she'd taken her hair down, making sure she looked like a well-used sex toy.

For the past hour, Damon and Marco had taken turns being onstage with her. They'd grabbed some of the faux toys the club performers used, but when the soft velvet strands of the flogger landed on her back she'd scream as if it were heavy leather.

Damon had turned her around after a stray blow with the fake flogger had landed on the all too real bruises left by the belt. That scream had been real, and from the look in his eyes, she knew he could tell the difference.

They'd *whipped* her breasts and belly, which were both protected by the corset. Someone had passed up a ball gag and blindfold, and after cleaning them, Marco had been all too happy to use them on her. Tasha was glad for the gag—moaning was a relief on her vocal cords after all the screaming.

Drool coated her chin, which she found disgusting but knew men found strangely attractive. Marco released the strap of the ball gag, and Tasha winced as she had to open her aching jaw wider for him to pull it out. She'd had it in for over a half hour—ten minutes longer than was recommended in consensual play. But she was a big girl, and some aspirin would ease her general aches.

She was sure she'd hurt a lot more if she weren't so ridiculously aroused. The play flogging had been pleasurable torture—no pain, just a hint of danger. Damon had even brought the flogger up between her legs a few times, the contact with her pussy enough that she hadn't had to fake her reaction. She'd loudly begged him to let her come, but he'd denied her, his eyes promising that as soon as they were out of here he'd finish what they'd started.

Marco passed her collar to Damon, who jerked on it. Tasha wasn't prepared and she tumbled off the stage into his arms.

"Sorry, baby," he whispered. "I didn't mean to be that rough."

"I'm just tired," she whispered. "It's okay."

"I just checked my email. There was another one from Sandra. She asked us to meet her tomorrow night—meaning tonight, at ten."

"I expected something like that." She tried to drop to her knees, but he wouldn't let her.

"No more," Damon said. "We're done. We're going home."

Home.

Tasha let Damon and Marco guide her out of the club. The limo was waiting at the curb. They piled in. Tasha took a seat but immediately regretted it and instead knelt on the floor. Weariness settled over her. She ached, she wanted to shower and she was worried.

Marco took a seat, caging her between his knees. "Come here," he demanded, pulling her leash. Tasha obediently kissed him.

She was tired, more tired than she should have been. She wasn't used to the emotional turmoil she'd been through this week, and it had eaten away at her stamina. She let her training take over, distancing herself emotionally and mentally—taking a break even as her hands dropped to Marco's fly, unzipping it and pulling his cock out.

"What the hell are you doing?" Damon demanded.

"Come here," Marco said, voice rough with desire. "I'm going to kiss you while she sucks my cock."

Tasha traced his dick from the tip to where it disappeared into his pants. She rubbed the vein on the underside and then toyed with the foreskin, listening to Marco's reaction and identifying his preferences. He liked having the underside of his cock stimulated.

"Marco, you ass. Look at her."

Tasha bent, mouth open, prepared to pleasure him.

Hands on her shoulders stopped her.

"Please, Master, let your slave pleasure you. If I do a bad job you can punish me. I'd deserve it." She didn't even think about what she was saying. The words were there, lines in a play she knew by heart.

"Oh God." Marco slid away from her. "I didn't...I'm sorry. Beautiful, I'm so sorry."

Tasha blinked in confusion. That wasn't what came next.

"Tasha, baby, look at me." Hands cupped her face. Damon's gold-green eyes searched her face. "Tasha, it's us. Come back from wherever you just went."

She shook her head. "I...Damon?"

With a snap, she popped back into herself. Weariness slammed down on her. She whimpered as each ache and pain made itself known.

"Get this shit off her." Damon unlocked the collar and flung it away. Marco undid the cuffs.

Embarrassment flooded her as she realized what she'd done. "I'm so sorry. I'm just tired. I needed to disengage for a second."

"Don't apologize," Marco said. "I'm the one who's sorry. I should have seen that you were hurting. Fuck, I'm an ass."

"Yes, you are." Damon gathered Tasha into his arms.

Tasha could feel his erection against her hip. "Let me take care of you." She tried to slide her hand between them to rub Damon's cock.

"No. Tasha, stop. You're not our submissive, our slave. That was just a game we were playing—a game we were really into."

"It's just us now," Marco whispered, rubbing her legs. "There's plenty of time to have sex. We have the rest of our lives. There's no rush. I want you to be happy. I want you to feel safe."

She closed her eyes and a tear escaped. "I'm just tired. I should be able to handle this."

"You don't need to. All you need right now is to let us take care of you."

When the limo stopped, Marco helped her into her coat and Damon carried her all the way to the condo. He didn't stop at the front door and took her right to the shower. Marco turned the water on in the master bathroom shower and cradled her as Damon shucked his clothing and climbed in. Tasha gasped as they urged her into the shower in her clothes.

Marco's blue eyes were shadowed as he watched Damon stripping the now-wet coat off her. "I'll go get us something to eat."

"Why is he leaving?" she asked.

"He feels guilty. He should."

"Why? I asked him to use the belt."

"Not for that. For not realizing that you were hurting and needed him to stop treating you like a sex toy."

Tasha lifted her arms as Damon struggled with the corset. She was pretty sure he was ripping it trying to get it off, but she didn't care.

"It can be hard to remember what's a game and what's real," she soothed.

"I want you to be real." Damon was drenched, his blond hair plastered to his head. Water ran over his muscles in a way she found inexplicably fascinating. "I want the real Tasha, not someone playing a part."

"I can't promise that," she whispered. "Sometimes it's easier to play a game."

"I know, baby. Just be honest with me." He hooked his fingers in the already ruined fishnet shirt and ripped it open. The tattered pieces slid off her arms and landed with a plop on the shower floor.

Finally, he eased the panties off her.

Honest.

Tasha looked down at his wet head. "Damon?"

"Yes?" He rose to his feet and dumped some soap into his hand. Starting with her arms, he washed her, the touch matter of fact, not arousing...but her body thrummed with desire.

"I...I want you to..." She swallowed, feeling like an idiot. She shouldn't say anything—just wait for them to go to sleep and then take care of herself.

"What do you want?"

"I want you to touch me. But I don't." Tasha shook her head. "I'm too tired to make sense."

Damon's hands stilled for a moment and then continued stroking her. "I understand."

She ducked under the stream to wash her face and then stepped out into the towel he held for her. Damon wrapped her up and then carried her from the bathroom to the master bedroom. He laid her down on the bed and then lay beside her.

He dipped his hand under the edge of the towel.

"Damon?"

"Let me take care of you."

His fingers found her pussy. Tasha sighed in pleasure and relief as he touched her clit. She was still wrapped up in the towel, her body warm and secure. Damon kissed her nose, her lips, her forehead. It was a gentle, almost nurturing touch as he circled her clit in a steady rhythm. Within minutes, she was breathing deep, and when the pressure within her reached its peak and the orgasm washed over her, Damon didn't push her. He pressed his palm against her pussy and held her throbbing sex as she came.

"Wow," Tasha whispered. "I didn't know it could be like that." She closed her eyes.

"Get some sleep, baby."

There were things she needed to do, but for now sleep seemed like a good thing.

MARCO STOOD in the door to his bedroom and watched Damon kiss and touch their wife. Her gentle cry as she came was a beautiful sound. She trustingly curled into Damon as she closed her eyes. He waited for a minute before he slid off the bed.

Their gazes met, but Marco looked away. Back in the kitchen, he started assembling sandwiches.

"Marco."

He didn't acknowledge Damon.

"Marco." Damon grabbed him and forced him to turn. "What the hell?"

"What?" Marco tried to hide his anger.

"What's wrong?"

"Nothing."

"You're jealous."

Marco jerked open the fridge door and stared into the white depths. He didn't know what he was looking for.

"Marco, you can't be jealous of Tasha and I being together—that will kill our relationship before it starts. We all have to accept there will be times when the other two will have sex. We can't be together all the time."

"That's not why I'm jealous," he ground out.

"Why then?"

"She trusts you. She doesn't trust me."

Marco was tired and a little drunk. In the sober light of day he wouldn't have admitted to such unflattering feelings, but right now he was angry and upset and couldn't hold that in. Slamming the fridge closed, he looked at his friend.

"I'm the one who protected her first, not you. I never wanted her hurt, and you were okay with it. I'm the one she should want comforting her."

Damon's shock was clear on his face before it morphed to anger. "I see. So who was I going to be in our trinity? The asshole she couldn't stand? Do you expect us to both love you and only you?"

Marco swallowed. Is that what he'd expected?

"Fuck you, Marco." Damon left the kitchen and the guest bedroom door slammed a moment later.

Marco took a tumbler from the counter and flung it across the room. The shattering of crystal didn't make him feel better.

DAMON JERKED AWAKE, sitting bolt upright. It felt like he'd only been asleep for a few hours, and he wasn't sure why he was awake now.

"Damon, you need to go."

Tasha appeared from the shadows. She was dressed in leggings and a sweatshirt, her hair back in a ponytail.

"What happened?" he asked, struggling to process what was going on. It wasn't yet seven and he had been asleep for less than three hours.

"Nothing. I should have told you last night, you need to go home."

"What are you talking about?"

"You need to go back to L.A. Today. Go out to dinner tonight. You need to be seen."

"Tasha…I just got to sleep."

"I packed your bag and booked you a flight. The cab will be here in twenty minutes."

"Why?" he groaned.

"Because if you're in L.A. then you can't be here murdering someone tonight."

With that, she turned and walked out of the room.

AN HOUR LATER, Damon was at O'Hare Airport, yawning as he went through security. He collapsed into a chair in the first-class lounge. He hadn't gotten to ask Tasha who she thought was getting murdered and hadn't had a chance to tell her about what Marco had said last night.

He was still pissed at his friend, though he knew better than to hold something said after a long, emotional day against Marco.

When he was on board, he tossed a blanket over himself, begged the flight attendant to let him sleep, and finally got some rest. He dreamed of them—Tasha and Marco. It started off sexy but quickly morphed into a nightmare that ended with him standing over Tasha's dead body.

At one, Tasha finished her Pilates routine and rose to her feet. She was still a bit sore and the belt marks had darkened to purple. She'd have to make sure Marco didn't see them.

He'd been sleeping on the couch when she woke Damon up and hustled him to the airport.

She went in search of water, but as soon as she left the guest bedroom she heard it—the first strains of music. Captivated, she went to the living room and curled up on the couch to listen.

He was beautiful when he played. As she watched his face, she realized that they had more in common than she'd thought—he had no choice but to live the music, to embody the sadness and joy in the notes. When he finished, he bowed his head, looking weary. That she understood. She knew exactly how hard it could be to take on extra emotions.

She applauded softly and he looked up.

"Tasha." He nodded stiffly.

"That was beautiful."

"I have rehearsal with the CSO—Chicago Symphony Orchestra—this week. I'm going in to practice the solo piece tonight."

Tasha frowned. "Is this a new part of your schedule?"

"No."

She filed that away—whoever had his phone would be able to see the rehearsals on his calendar, meaning that it could be used against him. "I'm sorry I took your bed last night."

Marco laid the bow to the strings and drew forth a low, ominous note. "I saw you together last night. You and Damon."

Tasha studied his profile. "Are you angry because he touched me? I know you love him."

"No. I'm angry because you wanted him and not me."

Tasha was shocked. He was jealous because she'd been with Damon, not because Damon had been with her? "But you love him," she said.

"I do. And I want you. I thought you and I...I thought there was something between us, and I hate myself for destroying it last night."

"You didn't destroy anything."

"How could I not have? You were hurt and exhausted. We kept you strapped to a damned cross for hours and yet the minute we were alone all I could think about was touching you, having you touch me."

"And why is that wrong?"

"Because I don't want to be like other men to you. I'm your husband." Marco put aside the cello, came to her and dropped to his knees. He took her hands in his. "I wanted to be the first one you loved. I know that's terrible, but that's what I wanted."

"You want me to love you?" Tasha's heart swelled and tears pricked her eyes

"Yes. Desperately."

"I'm so scared of falling in love with both of you. I don't know how to do this." Her voice wavered and she had to stop and bite her lip to fight back the tears. "Last night I was tired, and instead of telling you that, I turned my heart and mind off. I became what I'd only pretended to be up until that point—the perfect little slave girl."

"And I pushed you to that." Marco laid his head on her lap. "Forgive me."

Tasha let out a little sob. "Marco."

He rose, sat on the couch and cradled her against him. "I can be a selfish, conceited ass."

"And I can be a lot of things."

"We're quite the pair, aren't we?" He kissed her softly. "It's a good thing we have Damon."

"Yes, it is. I'm sorry about last night. I didn't mean to upset you."

"I'm the one who needs to apologize, and not just to you. I was an ass to Damon."

"He'll forgive you."

"And will you?"

"Only if you forgive me."

"Of course, beautiful." He kissed her softly.

Desire unfolded in her belly. Tasha pulled back. She wished there was time, but there wasn't. "I have to go."

"Where?" he asked, gaze hooded.

"I need to figure out what's going on. I think I can end this today. What time does your rehearsal finish?"

"Nine."

"Stay there. Keep other people with you if you can."

His gaze searched her face. "Alibi?"

"Yes." She slid reluctantly out of his arms.

"Tasha?"

"Yes?"

"Keep yourself safe. Whatever happens we'll deal with it. I'd rather do some jail time than see you get hurt."

"That's very sweet." She smiled. "It's also very stupid. You're lucky you're pretty."

Marco roared with laughter as she left the living room to get dressed. Tasha was smiling as she pulled on a black body-armor suit.

CHAPTER THIRTEEN

Tasha started on the roof of the club and then canvassed the area, moving in a spiral pattern. She'd put on jeans and a jacket and easily blended in with the late afternoon crowd on the streets. When she was done, she went back to the beginning and started again, each time identifying potential crime scenes.

If she was right, the failure of the blackmail scheme had caused the person behind it to up the ante. There was security footage of Marco and Damon in the alley last night meeting with a woman with dark hair. If a woman matching that was found dead, they would be suspects. The blackmail attempt and the video would come out in the investigation and Marco's travel to Las Vegas to look for her would seem sinister.

The email asking them to return to this area was an effort to get eyewitnesses who could place them around the body. Tasha was assuming that the murder would take place sometime today, and the video footage from the alley last night would have the date stamp changed. She suspected the plan had been to get Marco and Damon to chase the girl. When they caught up with her they'd find themselves standing over a still-warm dead body. The fact that Marco and Damon hadn't chased after the decoy, and then were heavily alibied in the club, meant the plan must have changed.

She'd gotten Damon out of harm's way—he was safely in L.A., and that meant that the security footage wouldn't work as a smoking gun for him, but it would establish that Marco and Damon knew the woman—even if only Marco had killed her. Even if Marco wasn't charged, the scandal of him being a person of interest might destroy both him and Damon.

For the next seven hours, Tasha roamed the city, checking the locations she'd identified earlier. It was nine fifteen. If they had access to Marco's schedule they'd assume he was done by now, meaning if anything was going to happen tonight it would be now.

Tasha slipped through the lobby of an office building, using a connecting door to enter the structure next door, then finally climbing fifteen flights of stairs to reach the roof and her chosen vantage point. There were two possibilities she could see from here.

A dark-haired man walked out of a shadowed doorway. He wore a suit and his head was bent. From a distance, his build and haircut were similar enough to Marco's that someone could mistakenly think it was him.

After a quick spike of adrenaline, Tasha forced herself to calm down. Cold settled around her like a cloak. Using the roofs and fire escapes as a highway, she went down half a block before dropping to street level. There was an alley that ran behind all the buildings on that side of the street. Tasha's feet were practically silent on the concrete and she slipped between the dumpsters.

The body was still warm. Dark hair blended with the shadows, but the face was undeniably that of the redhead. The dye job was recent—they'd forgotten to do her eyebrows, which were a pale red-gold.

There were four stab wounds across her belly just below her breasts. There was relatively little blood—she'd suffocated from punctured lungs. It was a bad way to die. Tasha had to accept that if she hadn't taken a long way around to get here the girl might still be alive.

She put latex gloves on over the leather ones she already wore and took a tiny flashlight from her pocket and used it to scan the area around the body. Marco's tie was a few feet away and speckled with blood. Tasha tucked it into her pocket. Checking the woman's coat, she found a few blond hairs—Damon's hair—that the decoy had grabbed last night. Inside the dead woman's coat pocket, she found a phone, which was undoubtedly Marco's.

She checked the scene again. The murder weapon was gone.

It was possible they'd gotten hold of a knife Marco had touched, but it was more than likely the real murder weapon was going to be planted on Marco's person or amongst his belongings. Tasha made her way back down the alley, using a service entrance to a hotel kitchen to escape unseen.

It was a race against time. She had to find that knife and make sure it couldn't be tied to Marco. The most obvious choice was the condo, followed by the Symphony Center. If she were the one planting the knife where would she go?

If she got this wrong, Marco's life could be over.

Tasha took off running.

MARCO'S FINGERS flew over the strings. His focus was absolute. The first-chair violinist stood with her eyes closed, her simple jeans and sweater nothing like the long black velvet gowns she wore for concerts. But it didn't matter what she wore, or what he wore. All that mattered was the music. Marco had stayed because of Tasha's instruction, and if she hadn't made the demand, he wouldn't be sitting on the nearly empty stage improvising with the first chair violinist. Music was his home, a place where he was grounded. He'd needed this.

Vivian's fingers were flying as she changed key and tempo. Marco followed her lead. On and on their song went. It didn't ever have to end.

There was a screech as the bow slid down the strings of the violin.

Marco looked up. "Vivian? You okay?"

"What's going on?" Using her bow as a pointer, she indicated stage right. Two guards were running while shouting into walkie-talkies.

Marco wasn't sure what to do and he was keenly aware of Tasha's instructions to make sure there was someone with him. Before he could decide if he wanted to investigate, the CSO manager hustled onstage.

"Marco, Vivian. You're both okay?"

"What's going on?"

"Someone broke in—actually, she broke in to your dressing room, Marco. One of the tech crew heard something and they found her when they went to check. We're calling the police."

"Her?" Marco rested his cello in its stand. "Where is she?"

Together, he and the manager hustled backstage, Vivian trailing behind them. Marco, as a guest—though he played with the CSO so much he was practically a member—had his own dressing room. Vivian and the conductor did also. The dressing rooms were down a short hall that contained the ticketing office and the electrical room.

Two security guards were dragging a figure out of his dressing room. "Careful, there's blood on her," one warned.

Marco's heart stopped when he saw who they held. Tasha was wearing a skin-tight black suit and her right hand was covered in blood.

"Wait." Marco rushed forward, brushing past the manager. "Leave her alone."

"Do you know her?" the manager asked.

Marco met Tasha's gaze. She shook her head slightly, but Marco ignored it. He wouldn't let them carry her to jail. "Yes," he said. "I do."

"You should have told me that there was someone stalking you." The manager looked worried. "I would have added more security."

Marco forced a laugh. "Stalking? Hardly. This is my girlfriend."

All eyes swiveled to him.

"Your girlfriend?" Vivian asked.

"Yes, this is my girlfriend...Natasha. She gets a bit pissed when I miss dinner reservations." Marco hoped he didn't sound as stupid as he felt. This was the lamest cover story in the world.

Tasha's eyes widened for a second, then she jerked free of the guards and threw her hands in the air. "You!" She pointed a bloody finger at Marco. "You think you can ignore me? Your music is more important?" She suddenly had a thick Russian accent. "Do you see this? I bleed for you. I cut myself coming to see you, but you are too busy, you do not even give them my name."

"Uh, Marco, are you sure she's not...uh." The manager was trying to find a polite way of asking if she was sane.

"She's a model," Marco blurted out. In his experience, the craziest ones were always models.

Tasha picked up this new piece and ran with it. "And you see what I've done?" She motioned to the all-black suit. "There's blood on it and dust. This is a new piece from Proenza Schouler. What will I tell Lazaro when he sees it? I wore it for you." Tasha ran her hands slowly down her sides, drawing everyone's attention to her body. "But you prefer the curves of the cello." She sneered. "I will find a man who appreciates me." She turned to the security guard who only minutes ago had been dragging her out. "You. You wish to fuck me?"

"Uh..."

Marco was biting his tongue to keep from laughing, but now it was time for him to do his part. Two could play the crazy card.

He grabbed her arm and jerked her forward. "I am the only man you'll fuck. And you will wait for me, always."

He cupped her head, wrapped an arm around her back and kissed her.

Someone cleared his throat, but Marco didn't stop. When he did eventually break the kiss, Tasha was panting. Only a guard, the manager and Vivian remained.

"An actual girlfriend?" Vivian asked. "Good for you, Marco. You need someone in your life." She touched the head of her bow to his shoulder. "I'll wait for opening night for proper introductions."

"You're sure you're okay?" The manager was looking at Tasha nervously.

She cuddled against Marco's side. "*Lyubov moya,* I'm sorry. But you know you cannot keep me waiting." She stuck out her lower lip in a pout and trailed her hands down his belly. She slipped her fingers under the waistband of his pants. Marco jerked in surprise. The manager and guard were both riveted.

"If you'll excuse me." The words were strangled as Marco tugged her hand out of his pants. "Can someone bring me my cello?" Marco herded Tasha to his dressing room. She was cooing at him in what sounded like Russian while she plucked at his clothing.

The instant the door closed, her face went blank and hard. "Lock the door and get the bag out of a garbage can."

"Tasha, what's going on?"

"Later."

Marco looked around his dressing room—everything seemed fine, except that his instrument case was open on the floor. A black coat lay in a heap on the floor, but it didn't look like the one Tasha had left in.

She knelt beside his cello case, peering at the black velvet lining. "The bag," she snapped.

Marco pulled the liner from the garbage can and passed it over. She wrapped it around her hand and reached in to the case, feeling along the edge.

"Got it," she said.

"Got what?"

She held up what she'd found—a steak knife. "The murder weapon."

Marco's vision darkened and he sat down. "Murder weapon? Who did you kill?"

Tasha folded the knife into the bag. "Do you take the cello home with you?"

"Yes. Tasha, who was murdered? Why was the knife in my case?"

"Good, I can deal with the blood when we get it to your condo." She went to the small couch across from the dressing table. Kneeling, she reached under it and pulled out a pair of black gloves and a small silver item about the length of a phone but only an inch wide.

"What's that?"

"My knife." She flicked a button and a blade shot out of the end. It was bloody. She wiped it clean with the gloves, careful not to touch it, and then put both into the garbage bag.

Reaching back under, she pulled out a tie and a cellphone, which she shoved into the bag. Finally, she bundled the jacket from the floor in on top of everything and twisted the bag closed. "I don't think he had time to plant anything but the knife, but look around. Tell me if you see anything out of place."

Marco looked around, but he was having trouble believing what he was seeing. "Why is there blood on your hand? Who was murdered? Who is *he*?"

Tasha stepped onto a chair and peered at the top of the wardrobe unit. "*He* is the man who murdered Sandra. She was stabbed with the knife that was in your case. He planted it there in order to frame you for murder. I followed him and we fought—that's why there's blood on my knife. That's his jacket."

"Did you kill him?"

"He ran. I stayed. I needed to distract them so no one would search your dressing room and find the knife."

There was a knock.

Tasha jumped off the chair, tousled her hair with her left hand and unzipped her bodysuit down to her bellybutton, letting it gape open to show the inner curves of her breasts. She grabbed Marco's shirt and yanked. Buttons went flying. "Answer the door."

In a daze, Marco unlocked and opened the door. The manager was cradling his cello. The proper older gentleman took one look at Marco's bare chest and ripped shirt and jerked his eyes to the ceiling.

"Here you go."

Marco opened the door enough to accept the cello. Tasha

had positioned herself on couch, and was trailing fingers up and down the bare triangle of flesh she'd exposed.

"*Lyubov moya*, come back to me."

"Would you call me a car?" Marco smiled weakly. "Thanks."

He took the cello and all but slammed the door in the manager's face.

"I thought my reputation with women couldn't get any worse. I was wrong." Marco sighed and laid the instrument into the case and closed it.

"You're the one who started it," Tasha said. There was a hint of anger in her words. "I would have been fine on my own."

"Beautiful, no, I'm sorry. I shouldn't have said that. I'm just a little freaked out." Marco reached for her but she turned away.

"How long until they bring you a car?"

"Ten minutes."

"That's okay. I can wait."

"Wait for what?"

"Doesn't matter." She tapped her fingers against her thigh in a steady rhythm. "I got the evidence he planted on the body, and you're now well alibied here. The assassin looked confused when he saw your jacket and the cello case—he didn't think you'd be here."

Marco took a minute to absorb what she was saying. This whole thing felt surreal. "Why bring the knife here?"

"Tomorrow an anonymous tip would be called in to the police saying you'd killed the woman whose body someone will find tonight or tomorrow morning. The police would search the condo first and then come here. They'd find the knife with her blood on it in your possession. If you'd left on time you would have had a less firm alibi for the time of the murder—an alibi that might be overlooked due to physical evidence. Your tie was near the body, your phone in her pocket. Damon's hair was on her coat.

"You'd be a suspect in the murder, your connection to Damon would come out in the investigation, and the resulting scandal would bring enough public attention to both of you that the Trinity Masters' secret would be in real jeopardy."

There was another knock and Tasha zipped her suit closed. She picked up the garbage bag and wrapped it in Marco's coat, which was draped over a chair.

She cocked her hips. "Let us go home and fuck like minks, *lyubov moya*."

"We're going to have a conversation about that accent." Marco murmured as he picked up the cello case. There was a wheel on the bottom. He propped the neck on his shoulder and opened the door. The security guard stationed outside looked vaguely disappointed when Tasha emerged fully dressed.

She walked beside him to the side door of the hall where an SUV was pulled up. The guard let them out and locked the door behind them.

"Let's go home." Marco put his cello in the back and climbed in beside her.

"Home," she said. "That sounds good."

"They were trying to frame me for murder," Marco told Damon.

Damon's face was a stony mask on the video call. "I doubt they would have been able to convict you, but it would have been an almighty scandal."

Marco nodded. The instant they'd walked in, Tasha had confiscated his cello case. She now had it open on the counter and was using a powder she called meat tenderizer to clean it.

Marco had tried to help but she'd stared him down until he retreated to the breakfast bar to place a video call to Damon.

"Go back to the part about Tasha and the fight," Damon said.

"Actually, I don't know much." Marco twisted his tablet so that Damon could see Tasha.

She was blotting the interior of the case with a paper towel. She held it up, inspected it and then nodded. She closed the case and fastened the buckles before taking it off the counter.

"What happened?" Marco asked.

She washed her hands and then moved the small box of supplies she'd retrieved from her luggage to the island. She upended the garbage bag they'd smuggled out of the Symphony Center on the granite. "When I found the body I cleaned up the scene. They had your hair, Damon, and Marco's tie from last night and his missing phone." She plucked the phone from the mess and set it aside. "I knew the assassin—who looked a bit like Marco—had at least a half an hour head start. I guessed that he would go to the Symphony Center and not come here."

She unzipped the top of her suit, and for a minute Marco lost track of what she was saying.

"I got in one of the emergency exits and found the dressing room. He was already there, looking at Marco's jacket and cello case. I think he realized there was something wrong. Marco shouldn't have been in the building.

"Before I could attack, he heard me. We fought. I went down for a moment and he planted the knife. We heard guards. He ran. I didn't want them looking around and finding the knife, so I stayed to be a distraction."

Wincing, she peeled the top of the suit off, pushing it down to her waist. Blood poured down her left side.

"Tasha!" Damon yelled

Marco jumped from the stool and ran to her, heart pounding. There was so much blood. "I'll call 911."

"No. Don't. I'll be fine." She winced and pressed a small medical pad to the injury. "The suit was keeping it from bleeding too much."

"The blood on your hand...it was yours."

"Yes."

Marco forced her arm up and examined the wound. It was a slice along her ribs that looked deep.

"You need stitches."

"I know."

"So we're going to the hospital."

Tasha rolled her eyes. "No, we're not. I'll do it myself."

"Take her to the hospital!" Damon demanded.

"Calm down and think," she snapped. "We can't. Marco, explain to him who you said I was."

Marco haltingly told Damon how he'd said she was his girlfriend Natasha, a model. "And then she started speaking Russian."

Damon rubbed his head. "She's right. No hospital. The police might get involved, and if they talked to anyone who was at the rehearsal they'll know you two had a fight. Instead of murder you might be charged with domestic abuse or assault."

Marco took a seat and watched as Tasha cleaned and disinfected the wound and then picked up a small packet containing a pre-packaged needle. He got her a mirror and sat in silence as she closed her wound with three small stitches. When she was done, Marco helped her bandage it.

"What do we do now?" Marco knew who Tasha was, knew what she could do, but somehow watching her calmly stitch herself closed brought home for him that she'd lived a life he would never really understand.

"I'm going to run a trace on the phone." Tasha's teeth were gritted and she was taking shallow breaths. "Both women involved in the original plot have been neutralized, as has the assassin." She took a bottle out of her kit, shook a pill out and swallowed it dry.

"But he got away."

"He won't get far."

"Did you put a tracker on him or something?" Marco saw her shiver. "Hold on, I'm going to get you a shirt."

He brought her a button-up shirt and then helped her slip into it. She thanked him and then asked him to get her computer. When he brought it over she hooked his stolen phone up and started tapping the keys.

"Tasha." Damon sounded worried. "How do you know he won't get far?"

"The blade of my knife was coated in sarin."

"Jesus," Damon breathed.

Marco looked at the screen. Damon's face was ashen. "What's sarin?"

"It's a highly illegal chemical weapon that is seriously dangerous to handle. Tasha, how do you have sarin? In large quantities it's considered a WMD. Even possessing it is enough to bring down UN sanctions and possible military action."

Marco looked at Tasha, expecting her to correct Damon. Surely she wouldn't carry a knife doused in something that dangerous. She ignored both of them. The skin on the back of Marco's neck prickled.

After what felt like an eternity of silence, she spoke. "The stab wound wasn't deep." She finished tapping the keys. "Marco, watch this."

"What am I looking for?" He took over the spot in front of the computer.

"The number of times the photos were downloaded from your phone."

Marco watched the scrolling lines of code, feeling like he was in the matrix. Tasha put on latex gloves and then picked up the leather gloves she'd shoved in the bag, turned and dumped them in the sink.

"Sarin is a nerve agent." She flicked the knife open, tipped what smelled like bleach out of a tiny bottle onto a gauze pad, and cleaned the blade. When she was done she threw the cotton pad into the sink. "In low levels it causes permanent neurological damage."

"So the guy you fought with...he's as good as dead," Damon said.

"Yes."

There was another beat of silence. Then Damon exploded. "Damn it, Tasha, what if he was just some random guy?"

Marco, too, was having a hard time understanding that she'd just effectively murdered someone. She seemed the same as she had before, as if this were all normal for her. Sometimes he forgot that it was.

She picked up the jacket and turned it inside out. "He wasn't some random guy. He knew how to kill Sandra, was very skilled in hand-to-hand combat and there are no tags in his clothes." She held up the jacket as proof.

"What does that have to do with anything?"

"Clothing can reveal more about a person than is safe. Anyone in the game would have tag-less items." She tossed the jacket into the sink with the gloves, tie and cotton pad and took a small vial from her kit.

"What's that?" Marco took his eyes off the computer for a moment to look at her.

"Chlorine triflouride. It's a weak form, but it's still one of the most flammable substances on earth." She upended the vial into the sink, lit a match and tossed it in.

Marco jumped back as a fireball whooshed its way up towards the ceiling. It dissipated, leaving a pile of ashes, which she quickly washed down the drain.

"Holy shit!" Marco scanned the ceiling, but nothing seemed to be on fire. "You just made a fireball. In my kitchen. Damon, is that legal?"

Damon had his head on his desk, so all Marco could see was his hair. He looked up and rubbed his face. "She poisoned a man with a substance which, if she had a gallon of it, would be considered a WMD. She just used a different substance, this one so dangerous that the Nazis refused to touch it, to destroy evidence."

"The computer," Tasha snapped at Marco.

Marco glanced at the screen. "I think it's done."

Tasha stripped off her gloves. She peered at the screen and then a grin spread across her face. "Got it." She wiggled out of the bottom of her cat suit, which was almost enough to distract Marco from the seriously dangerous and insane things she was doing.

"What did you get?"

"The photos were only downloaded once. There's no real way to tell how many times the files were moved after that—but I can use the details from the phone to tighten my digital net."

Tasha gathered up her computer and went to the dining room table.

Marco got her something to eat and sat with her as she worked on her computer. After an hour, she went to the bedroom and came back wearing shorts and fuzzy socks along with his shirt. Her glasses were perched on her nose. Marco stayed with her for another hour, but it didn't seem like there was anything he could do to help.

He dropped a kiss on her head and then went and stretched out on the couch.

IT WAS NEARLY three in the morning when she sat back and flexed her fingers.

"Done?"

Damon's voice startled her. She hadn't realized that Marco had left his tablet on the table, the screen facing her and the video call with Damon still active.

"You're still up," she said.

"It's not that late out here."

She took off her glasses and rubbed her eyes. She was hovering in that strange place between exhaustion and delight.

"You're smiling," Damon said. "Is that a good thing?"

"It is. Someone tried to send both the photos from Damon's phone and the video to the Chicago police as well as several Chicago reporters."

"Shit."

"No, it's a good thing. The net worked. Each file was corrupted, as were the source files in a cloud-sharing platform that some copies were being stored on. The messages will be blocked by the email clients, the text content is scrambled beyond recognition and anyone who did try to unscramble them or open the attachments would suffer from a serious OS malfunction."

"You did all that?"

"Yes."

"That's amazing."

The genuine admiration in his words had her smiling.

"Thank you. I also got some leads on where the files originated from."

"What do you mean?"

"My best guess is that Sandra and Jennie turned over the video and Marco's phone to someone here in Chicago. I can see an initial upload here. Then the files were transferred to a server. An IP address that's being cloaked logged in to that same server. I have to assume whoever that was copied or downloaded the images and video.

"It's that download, which happened only a day after the party, and weeks before the blackmail, that I need to ID. Whoever did that is probably the person who put Sandra and Jennie up to this in the first place. They arranged the blackmail and they were manipulating the whole situation. They killed Sandra and tried to have Jennie killed."

Tasha compiled her findings, ran them through an encoder and then uploaded them to a secure server that only the Grand Master and a few other members of the Trinity Masters had access to.

"I'm going to get some sleep, but I'll head out in the morning." She closed her computer and yawned.

"Go? Go where?"

"After whomever is behind this."

"No, Tasha. You won't. I meant what I said. You aren't going to do this anymore."

"Damon, I'm the only one who can—"

"Who can what? Hunt down this supervillian who tried to frame us?"

Tasha knew he was being sarcastic, but she replied, "Yes."

They'd woken Marco, who stumbled over to the table and laid his hands on Tasha's shoulders. "This whole time you've been able to see all the pieces—see how everything we did could and might be used against us."

"It's what I do."

"You're been beaten and stabbed. All for what? To protect our reputations? To protect the Trinity Masters? They're not worth this. We're not."

"That's not for you to decide." Tasha's words were quiet but firm. "To me, you are. I've suffered worse for people who never even knew I was there. I would die for both of you." Her lips trembled for a second, but then she pressed them together. "When I'm with you, either of you, I feel...I feel normal. I can tease you, and you tease me. You respect me and want to keep me safe even when that's stupid, yet you let me do what I need to."

She shivered and Marco bent and wrapped his arms around her.

"I don't know what love feels like," she whispered, looking at Damon while Marco cradled her, "but I don't think it could be better than this."

Marco met Damon's gaze and something passed between them—it would take a while for him to fully process what had almost happened to them, but for now what was important was that Tasha loved them, even if she didn't use that word. Marco loved her, and if the look on Damon's face was any indication, he loved her too.

A FEW HOURS LATER, Tasha slipped out of bed. Despite their conversation last night, she had no intention of dropping this. Her assignment had been to deal with the blackmailer and to keep the Trinity Masters' secret from getting out. She'd done that—both women involved were effectively neutralized. Sandra was dead and Jennie was so addled from drugs that Tasha doubted she remembered what she'd done. It also meant she wasn't going to be of any help in identifying the person who'd paid five thousand dollars a pop to keep her on payroll at the BDSM club. It was entirely possible that once Jennie went to prison she'd be killed.

Unable to send the video of photos to anyone, and without the women who could testify as to the authenticity of the video, the person who'd orchestrated this was out of options. He could mail jump drives or CDs with the files, but that was risky—physical storage mediums were like tags in clothing. They said a lot.

The issue of Damon and Mark wearing matching rings on the video was moot. Whoever was behind this already knew about the Trinity Masters. Already knew far more about the secret society than Tasha was comfortable with. That's why she had to go. If she was going to track this person down, she had to do it now.

A square of white rested on the carpet just inside the door.

Tasha backed into the kitchen, took some gloves out of her bag, pulled the neck of her shirt up over her nose and mouth and inched down the hall.

Crouching, she picked up the envelope. It was greeting-card size and made of thick ivory paper. Tasha frowned. She'd seen this type of envelope before—in the Grand Master's office.

Tugging down her shirt, she shifted to sit on the floor, turning the envelope over in her hands. Sliding her thumb under the flap, she opened it and removed the plain card inside. The front was blank, and the inside contained a brief hand-written message.

Be happy, Tasha. This is my fight.

—Harrison

Tasha pressed her fingers over her lips as the first tears fell. After a minute, a small laugh escaped her. She tipped her head back against the wall and hugged the letter to her chest. Sitting on the floor in the dark, Tasha let go. Her husbands were safe, and for her that was enough. She could, and would, leave the rest of this battle to others.

She went back to the bedroom, stripped out of her clothes and slid in beside Marco, who pulled her against his chest. Tasha laid her cheek against his warm skin, closed her eyes and went back to sleep.

CHAPTER FOURTEEN

The Grand Master had given them a month to return and be formally married. They didn't wait that long.

A week after Tasha had thwarted the blackmail attempt and stopped Marco from being framed for murder, when they were sure the police weren't looking for Marco, they met in Boston.

Damon still didn't understand who'd been behind all this—Tasha didn't know or wouldn't say, but with each day that passed he grew less and less concerned. He was relieved that his stupidity hadn't nearly led to the outing of the Trinity Masters, and frustrated that he and Marco had been used as pawns in a larger scheme. But those were things he and his soon-to-be spouses couldn't and shouldn't have to deal with.

He'd flown to Boston on his own, meeting them there. Tasha had stayed in Chicago the past week, attending some of Marco's additional rehearsals as Natasha the Russian girlfriend.

It had been lonely in L.A. by himself, but he spoke with them often. Tonight he would see them, touch them again.

They gathered in the ceremony room, each anonymous in their robes until the Grand Master appeared and ordered them to push back their hoods. Tasha smiled when she saw him and Damon couldn't help the answering smile from curving his lips. Her hair was silvery gold in the cool lights that surrounded the altar. She made him feel young and untried when in reality he was jaded and hard. After the ceremony, they'd go to the honeymoon suite of a hotel, where, for the first time, they'd fully engage each other sexually. Damon's cock twitched. He transferred his attention to Marco.

Marco looked like an alchemist or some dark sorcerer. The black hood pooled on his shoulders and his hair brushed his forehead. Damon had to look away before his erection got out of control.

"Join me," the Grand Master said.

Together they made their vows. The ceremony held no legal standing, and yet was far more binding than anything the outside world had. There was no divorce among the Trinity Masters. They were bound for life.

TASHA CROSSED her arms and then uncrossed them. She started to take a seat on the couch and then sprang up again. She'd been taught and trained how to handle any situation, but for the first time in her adult life, she had no idea what to do.

They were in a suite in a hotel not far from the Boston Library. The Grand Master had offered them each a separate room connected by a living area, but they'd declined, opting to take only the large honeymoon suite. Marco and Damon were bringing their things up from the car, and, she suspected, going over their plan.

She'd caught snippets of conversation over the past week,

and knew they'd been planning their seduction of her. It was sweet and thoughtful—something men did for women who baked pies and wore floral prints. Not women who had knife fights.

The wound in her side had started to heal and the bruise on her face was gone. Faint purple lines still marked her ass, but she hoped it wouldn't derail them.

Hugging herself, she went to the bar in the living area. It was fully stocked. Wanting something to do, she made vodka martinis. The door opened just as she was pouring.

The guys left the bags by the door. Marco wore black slacks and a dove-gray shirt. Damon had on a black suit, white shirt and black tie. It was almost a tux, as if he'd dressed for a wedding. The effort was wasted since the ceremony demanded they wear robes, but Tasha understood the impulse. She was wearing a tea-length white dress with a collarbone-bearing neckline. There was tulle in the skirt, giving it body and accentuating the retro style. The dress wasn't practical—it would be hard to fight in and wasn't overtly sexual enough to help her manipulate anyone.

She'd stood in the store for an hour before buying it, terrified. No amount of explanation would be able to make Marco and Damon understand that in this pretty dress she felt unarmed and vulnerable. She wouldn't have worn it for anyone but them.

Marco sauntered over, accepting the martini she handed him. He kissed her softly before taking a sip.

"What a good little wife we have, Damon. She has our drinks waiting for us."

Damon laid a hand on her back and kissed her cheek before accepting his drink. "You would deserve it if she kicked your ass."

"I can't help it. She looks wifely in that dress."

"Wifely." Tasha had a bad feeling she was blushing. She could control her reaction if she wanted to, but she didn't—she didn't have to. "Well, you both look husbandly."

They raised their glasses in a silent toast. Tasha took a sip and then set her glass down. Her fingers were shaking. They were standing close to her, crowding her against the bar.

She wanted to grab and kiss them, to move past this nervous anticipation and have their hands on her, but at the same time she was terrified.

Committing to this trinity was the most dangerous thing she'd ever done. It was a lifetime commitment, when previously she hadn't let herself think about the future. Why would she? Eventually one of her ops would have killed her.

She took a seat at the baby grand piano in the corner. Unlike Marco's natural-wood-toned one, it was shiny black lacquer. She caught sight of her reflection and almost didn't recognize herself. Her hair was in a bun and the dress made her look soft and feminine. Is this who she was now?

She touched the keys, not pressing any of them. She'd always wanted to learn to play, but an instrument required regular practice and she'd never managed it.

Marco slid onto the bench beside her. She started to get up but he urged her to stay.

"Give me your hands."

Tasha let him position her fingers on the keys. He leaned close as he whispered in her ear. "This is middle C. Use your thumb."

She tentatively pressed down. A clear note sounded from the belly of the piano.

"Now your middle finger. And your pinky."

Following his instructions she played one note at a time.

"Good," he said. "Keep going in that pattern." Marco put his own hands on the keys and started to play.

A smile curved her lips. "It's *Heart and Soul*."

"It is." He answered her smile, still playing.

"*Heart and Soul?*" Damon came up behind them, laying a hand on each of their shoulders. "That sounds right. You're now my heart and soul."

Tasha's fingers slipped from the piano keys. Damon tipped her head back, bent and kissed her. It was firm, bordering on demanding. As his tongue swept into her mouth, Marco took her hands from her lap and kissed her palms.

"Are you ready to move to the bedroom?" Marco asked.

Damon offered Tasha his arm, escorting them to the large, lush bedroom. The bed was huge, and it was a good thing because they'd need the space.

"Tonight we have a plan," Marco told her.

She nodded once, clinging to Damon's arm.

"If you get scared, don't lock yourself away. Tell us."

"I will," she whispered.

Then they were both there, hands roaming her body, lips on hers. They took turns kissing her. She was breathless as Damon unzipped her dress. She wasn't wearing a bra, but she heard him chuckle when he saw her panties.

"It's stupid I know," she whispered, embarrassed.

"I like it," Damon said, turning her so that Marco could see her white lace panties with the word *bride* spelled out in rhinestones on the ass.

"Hmm, I'm not sure." Marco's hand slid down her belly. "Let me check." He rubbed his fingers over the lace covering her mound and then pressed between her legs. "Oh yes," he said as Tasha's head fell back. "They're very nice."

Damon carried her to the bed. She pulled the pins from her hair, watching as they undressed. Marco's movements were smooth and quick, while Damon was more deliberate, each button and zip given careful attention.

Marco's cock was hard, jutting up from the nest of dark hair. He joined her on the bed, urging her to lie down. Tasha reached for her panties but he stopped her.

"Leave them on."

He settled beside her, his left hand roaming over her chest. He was gentle to start, thumbing her nipples and cupping her breasts, but his touch quickly became more intense. He took a nipple between thumb and finger and pinched it hard enough to have her gasp, then he tugged.

Damon was finally naked—his cock was shorter but thicker than Marco's. He spread her legs, settling between them on his belly. He traced the seam in the center of her lace panties, pushing the fabric into her pussy until she was lifting her hips.

"Wait," she begged. "Let me touch you."

"Not this time. Let us do this for you."

"But I won't be able to hold on. I'm already close. You make me...you make me..." Tasha couldn't finish the sentence, didn't even remember what she'd wanted to say. Damon's mouth was on her pussy, his teeth scraping her clit through the lace. Marco bit and suckled her nipples as he slid a hand under her head and took a fistful of her hair.

Tasha clung to the sheets, but then grabbed her husbands, her nails in Marco's chest, her fingers pressing Damon's head tighter against her.

Damon pulled the panties to the side, his tongue making contact with her clit.

Tasha screamed, her whole body arching as she came. Pleasure tingled along all her nerves and she was only vaguely aware of Damon tugging her panties off.

"Tasha, look at him, look at Damon," Marco urged.

She opened her eyes to see that Damon was positioned between her thighs, his cock hard and glistening. She licked her lips and looked between them.

"If you need more time." Damon's teeth were gritted, garbling the words.

"I...I'm ready," she whispered.

Damon guided the head of his cock to the entrance of her body. Marco hooked an arm under her left knee, pulling it up and opening her further. Damon slid in another inch.

It was glorious. Part of Tasha had been afraid that after all this waiting, penetration by a penis would not be any different than the dildos or vibrators she'd used and had been used on her before.

It was different, gloriously different.

She'd already come and her body was tight from the orgasm. She acutely felt his cock opening her, pressing against her internal walls. Marco was watching them, his gaze roaming their naked bodies before fixing on the point where Damon's cock disappeared inside her. Having him watch, feeling his cock rubbing her hip, added another layer to her arousal.

Marco moved, releasing her leg, and Damon braced his elbows on either side of her. Tasha ran her hands through his hair and stroked his shoulders.

"You feel good inside me. I wasn't expecting to like it this much."

Damon's gaze was molten gold. "It's never been like this for me either. It's never felt so important."

Tasha looked over Damon's shoulder at Marco, who'd returned to the bed holding condoms and lube.

She looked between them. "You're going to fuck Damon?"

"Yes. I'm going to fuck him while he fucks you. Then we'll switch. Then we'll both fuck you."

Tasha shuddered in arousal, but Damon looked nervous.

"Are you okay?" she asked him.

"Yes." He dropped his head to her shoulder. "I guess I'm not going to be a virgin anymore either," he muttered.

Tasha kissed his shoulder, cradling his hips as he rocked gently inside of her. She watched as Marco put on a condom and then a glove before opening the lube.

Damon stilled above her. Taking his face in her hands, Tasha kissed him. She knew the moment Marco's fingers entered his ass by the way he flinched. A moment later, he was moaning into her mouth. Another flinch and he ripped his lips away from hers. His teeth closed over her shoulder.

Tasha gasped, clinging to Damon.

"I'm sorry," he murmured.

"Don't be. I like it."

"Are you ready?" Marco ran his hands over Damon's back.

"Yes," he growled.

Tasha lifted her head to watch as Marco pressed his cock into Damon. Once he was seated, they were still, joined in a way Tasha had never expected. She could feel Damon's cock twitching inside her.

It felt amazing—kinky and decadent while at the same time safe. She sank into the feeling, reveling in it, but soon that wasn't enough. She wiggled her hips, but though Damon kept his weight off her, there was no way Tasha could move their combined mass.

"Move," she begged.

As if that was what they'd been waiting for, the men shifted. Marco withdrew and then Damon did the same—fucking himself back onto Marco's cock. When Tasha realized that in order to thrust into her Damon had to fuck himself on Marco, her arousal spiked. There was something delicious about making Damon, who was so controlled and dominant, helpless.

From the look on Marco's face, she could tell he felt the same.

Damon found his rhythm, and soon Tasha couldn't think

about anything else but his cock sliding into her. She was owned, loved, and yet she also possessed them. She also loved them.

The second orgasm built slowly, curling in her belly like a snake. She clawed at Damon's back, demanding he fuck her, demanding Marco fuck Damon harder, wanting to feel the combined force of their bodies.

"I'm going to come," Damon growled against her shoulder. He turned his head, capturing her mouth in a brutal kiss as he slammed into her and held the position. Tasha was close, teetering on the edge. She was about to beg Damon to keep going when Marco started to move.

He slammed into Damon, the force of it grinding Damon's hips against her. Tasha screamed as friction on her clit sent her over the edge. She returned Damon's brutal kiss as the orgasm ripped through her.

Marco's teeth were gritted as he fucked Damon's ass until he too came.

They collapsed in a sweaty, panting tangle, one man on each side of her.

"I love you." Tasha closed her eyes. She hadn't meant to say it—she wasn't even sure it was true. But this swelling feeling inside her needed a name, and love was her best guess.

"I love you too, beautiful." Marco kissed her gently.

Damon's fingers were on her chin, turning her from Marco's kiss so that he could have her lips. "I love you, baby."

They lay that way for a long time, silent and content.

"WE NEED A PLAN." Tasha picked a chocolate-covered strawberry off the plate and bit into it.

"I have a plan. That's why you're wearing a plug." Damon licked the strawberry juice from her lips.

She shifted, leaning against him. The plug they'd used to tease her before dinner was firmly embedded in her ass. It was hardly her first time wearing one, but it was the first time it had made her this aroused.

Though she was lounging in a white silk robe—found in the bridal lingerie section—she might as well have been naked. Damon kept slipping his hand under the fabric to play with her nipples. Rather than making her feel like an object, it made her feel wanton. If Damon's semi-erect penis was any indication, he too was riding a low level of arousal.

"If you were a good husband you'd be more accepting of a nice ass fucking," Marco said as he popped open the second bottle of champagne.

"I'm more than happy to fuck both of you that way."

Tasha's lips twitched. "You're a bit of a prude," she teased him.

"That's hardly true. If we used the legal standard of a reasonable person—"

"No legal standards. Spare me." Marco poured the champagne.

"By a reasonable person's standards," Damon said loudly, "regularly participating in orgies, going to sex clubs and marrying both a man and a woman, at the same time, is hardly prudish."

"Therefore you're allowed to say you'll only do the fucking and not get fucked?" Marco handed Tasha a glass and winked.

"You're damned right," Damon muttered.

Tasha lost the battle to hold back her laughter.

Marco sat on her other side and pulled one of her feet onto his lap.

She cuddled against them. It was hard to decide what she

wanted more—to continue the sweet intimacy they'd shared while dining on room service, or for them to return to the bedroom to continue learning how they fit together. The plug was the preparation for what was coming next—Tasha couldn't wait to be between them, their big hard bodies surrounding hers as she took one man in her pussy and the other in her ass. Once the thought had scared her—not so much the physical act, but what it would mean. Now it was almost all she could think about. It was unbearably sweet that they'd planned it all out and had a plug ready to help prepare her for the double penetration. Tasha wasn't entirely sure a normal woman would think being made to wear a butt plug was sweet, but for her it was.

Tasha rubbed her toes over the front of Marco's pants. His cock stiffed under the sole of her foot.

"Shall we go to the bedroom?" she whispered. Damon's hand tightened on her breast and Tasha moaned.

"I like that plan," Damon said. "Come on, husband, wife." Marco rose and then held out his hands to pull them to their feet.

EPILOGUE

Harrison leaned back and sighed heavily, awaiting the inevitable meeting. He'd sat in the Grand Master's chair for nearly a decade, inheriting the prominent position from his father. The Trinity Masters was more than a club to him. More than a way of life. It was in his blood. The strictures and philosophies of the secret society were his religion. He believed in them, trusted that what the founding fathers had put in place two centuries earlier was as vital to the success of the country as The Constitution. The members had a responsibility to use their intelligence, their drive, their talents—even their fortunes—for good and progress. It was—in fact—their God-given duty.

For two hundred years, his family had preserved the society, protected their values, kept the organization safe and strong. And now, he was failing them all.

Someone not within the Trinity Masters had uncovered their existence. Given the blackmail video made of Marco and Damon, it was clear their motives weren't good. Exposure would bring the downfall of the society, reveal members' identities, destroy them.

Harrison had excused Tasha from the task of hunting down their enemy, despite the fact she was perhaps their best weapon. He refused to pull the young woman back into a life she'd never chosen. She was only beginning to find herself—the true Tasha—with her husbands. Harrison enjoyed watching her come into her own. He wouldn't take that from her...not even for the Trinity Masters.

So it fell to him.

He needed to find the villain on his own and bring him down. And he needed to do it quickly and quietly—without alerting the membership.

Unfortunately, he was facing another problem, one of his own making.

Michael and Price were on their way. Though he stood as the controlling force behind the secret society, no leader stands alone. Michael and Price were his conscience, his sounding boards. Sometimes they were his voice of reason.

Today, however, they weren't coming to guide him, but to issue an ultimatum.

Not even the Grand Master was exempt from the Trinity Masters' laws. And though he'd put this moment off as long as he could, time had finally run out.

Harrison needed to choose his mates and marry.

The next triad he formed would be his own.

Though the mystery in Scorching Desire was resolved, there was more to Tasha, Damon and Marco's story. We wanted to know how these three complicated, powerful people were going to make their relationship work. The short story, After Burn, answers that question and picks up the night of their wedding, a few hours after we last saw them. Download your free copy HERE.

AND DON'T STOP THERE! Harrison, the Grand Master is heading for a fall. Forbidden Legacy is available now.

READ THE ENTIRE TRINITY MASTERS: Fall of the Grand Master
- Elemental Pleasure
- Primal Passion
- Scorching Desire
- Forbidden Legacy

AND CHECK out these other series...all part of the Trinity Masters world.

SECRETS AND SIN
- Hidden Devotion
- Elegant Seduction
- Secret Scandal
- Delicate Ties
- Beloved Sacrifice
- Masterful Truth

MASTERS ADMIRALTY
- Treachery's Devotion
- Loyalty's Betrayal

Pleasure's Fury
Honor's Revenge
Bravery's Sin

THE HAYDEN BROTHERS
Fiery Surrender
Necessary Pursuit
Joyful Engagement (a novella)
Wrath's Storm

THE MAFIA
Suspicion's Fire
Desire's Addiction
Danger's Heir

WARRIOR SCHOLARS
Hollywood Lies

CALLING ALL FACEBOOKERS! Did you know there's a group for fans of the Trinity Masters series? Come join Mari and Lila for behind-the-scenes stories, contests, exclusive sneak peeks, and hilarious text threads. Join the society right HERE.

TURN the page to read the prologue of Forbidden Legacy.

FORBIDDEN LEGACY

P rologue

THE YOUNG MAN in the shadows stood a fair distance from the mourners, studying everyone who approached the widower. He lifted his camera and focused his long-range lens, zooming in until he had a clear shot of faces...and hands.

Hands, he had come to discover, told him more than faces. One of the gentlemen reached out to the widower, lifting his left hand to place it in a consoling fashion on the grieving man's shoulder.

The young man snapped a picture and then looked in the viewfinder. A smile crossed his face. The ring. The symbol. It was there.

"Gotcha." Another piece to the puzzle. Another fly captured in the web. He had been studying the symbol for nearly a year, tying it to a slew of rich and powerful people from current day all the way back to the American Revolution. While its significance wasn't quite clear to him yet, he was close to discovering the secret. And he knew it was big.

He lifted the camera once more and snapped a few more shots of the dark-haired man. He'd upload the photos to his laptop at the hotel and run a facial-recognition scan using the hacker software he'd designed. By tonight, he'd have this man's name and life story.

He studied the other people around the two caskets. Everyone at the small ceremony had an air about them—of wealth, position, power. His mother used to warn him about these sorts of people, claiming they were the wolves in sheep's clothing, the ones to look out for. She'd had a good reason to believe that. Two of the wolves at this funeral had destroyed her life—and his. He was going to ensure they paid for it. Dearly.

Thoughts of his mother sent a surge of anger through him. He took a deep breath, finding a way to turn the heat to cool, the frustration to calculation. The villains were here in Boston and the means for their destruction were at hand. The first part of the punishment had already begun as he looked at the two caskets. His handiwork. The dead women were merely pawns in his game, and their deaths had certainly paid off.

He glanced at the widower, taking in his hunched posture. The man's pain was almost tangible. The young man grinned. He intended to exploit that grief, turn it to his advantage. The widower was devastated, weakened by the loss. It would take very little effort to push the man completely over the edge and finish him off. But before he did, he intended to get answers from him.

Then he'd have the weapons needed to destroy the mastermind. Dr. Harrison Adams would suffer for his sins.

Harrison moved in to offer his condolences to the widower.

His face was as familiar to him as his own. No picture was necessary. He had a whole wall full of shots of this bastard.

He had studied Harrison's face at length over the past year, and soon he would discover the means to obliterate him. An eye for an eye. Harrison would lose everything by the time the young man was finished.

At long last, the wait was almost over.

It was time to strike.

FORBIDDEN LEGACY IS AVAILABLE NOW.

ABOUT THE AUTHORS

Virginia native Mari Carr is a *New York Times* and *USA TODAY* bestseller of contemporary sexy romance novels. With over two million copies of her books sold, Mari was the winner of the Romance Writers of America's Passionate Plume for her novella, *Erotic Research*.

Join her newsletter so you don't miss new releases and for exclusive subscriber-only content. You can visit Mari's website at https://maricarr.com or email her at mari@maricarr.com.

Lila Dubois is an award winning author of erotic, paranormal and fantasy romance. Her book J is for..., the tenth book in the bestselling checklist series, won the 2019 National Readers' Choice Award. Additionally, she's been nominated for the RT Book Reviews Erotic Novella of the Year for Undone Rebel and the Golden Flogger.

Having spent extensive time in France, Egypt, Turkey, Ireland and England Lila speaks five languages, none of them (including English) fluently. Lila lives in California with her own Irish Farm Boy and loves receiving email from readers.

You can visit Lila's website at www.liladubois.net. She loves to hear from fans! Send an email to author@liladubois.net or join her newsletter.

Made in the USA
Las Vegas, NV
21 January 2026